7/2

Raffaella Barker is the author of *The Hook, Hens Dancing, Summertime, Green Grass, Phosphorescence* and *A Perfect Life.* She lives in Norfolk with her family.

Praise for Raffaella Barker:

'It should be read for the tranquillising effect of Barker's elegantly glittering prose and the gentle mockery that greets Venetia's endless domestic mishaps . . . a disarmingly wry and engaging narrator with a keen eye for nature and a shrewd insight into the follies of urban chic'
Financial Times

'A fine, spiky sense of humour' *Daily Telegraph*

'I loved it. I couldn't put it down . . . Raffaella Barker is so good at drawing her characters and making them likable that within about ten pages you feel you know them intimately'
Daily Express

'An engaging work, sewn up with a dry line in wit'
Scotland on Sunday

'She writes beautifully, gathering intensity . . . combining, with apparent ease, emotion and admirable precision'
Independent

'Raffaella Barker is a writer of talent' *Times Literary Supplement*

'This charming novel overflows with eccentric characters . . . a satisfying mix of entertaining domestic disasters and musings on kitten heels, hens and new love' *Daily Mail*

'Her writing and characters are beautifully formed and controlled with inconsequential moments adding to the charm . . . pure therapy: Barker's books are good for you'
Country Life

'A light, bright and optimistic read . . . throw yourself down on the sand, dive between those silken sheets or luxuriate on the shag-pile, and enjoy it – I certainly did' *Literary Review*

COME AND TELL ME
SOME LIES

Raffaella Barker

headline
review

First published in Great Britain in 1994
by Hamish Hamilton

First published in 2000 by Review
An imprint of HEADLINE BOOK PUBLISHING

This paperback printed in 2006 by HEADLINE REVIEW
An imprint of HEADLINE BOOK PUBLISHING

A HEADLINE REVIEW paperback

3

ISBN 0 7472 6481 3

Typeset in Galliard by Palimpsest Book Production Limited,
Polmont, Stirlingshire

Printed and bound in Great Britain by
Clays Ltd, St Ives plc

Headline's policy is to use papers that are natural, renewable and
recyclable products and made from wood grown in sustainable
forests. The logging and manufacturing processes are expected to
conform to the environmental regulations of the country of origin.

HEADLINE BOOK PUBLISHING
A division of Hodder Headline
338 Euston Road
London NW1 3BH

www.reviewbooks.co.uk
www.hodderheadline.com

For my father and my mother

My father believed in angels. He named me after one of the archangels and in honour of an Italian Contessa called Gabriella who wore emeralds on every finger and lived in a Renaissance villa overlooking Lake Nemi. The Contessa found him charming and became his patroness: 'You are a famous poet. You will write your greatest work here in Italy,' she insisted, and she gave him a little cottage in her garden. A friend, a young painter called Graham Kingsley, sent him a telegram: 'Patrick, I'm bringing you a present.' My father wrote back, 'To hell with the present. Bring me a future.'

Kingsley arrived with my mother, Eleanor. She was twenty-two and wore straw hats; she had black hair and luminous white skin. She skulked in the shade of the hot Italian summer dreaming of Scottish moors, mauve skies and rain. Kingsley left after three days. Eleanor stayed for ever. She was Patrick's future, and she had brought her wellington boots.

The myths of my family, favourite fables told again and again, are brought out like battered photographs, nostalgia-scented and made alive by scrambled memory. They are fairy-tales, fantasies grown from a seed of truth into something wild and overblown. Only the house, Mildney, and the five children – me, then Brodie, Flook, Dan and finally Poppy – remain as constants in my mind. And of course, my parents, Patrick and Eleanor. The lives they led before I was born move in my head with my own memories until I cannot distinguish truth from legend. Perhaps there is no difference.

Patrick loved memories and myths. He leaned his elbows on the arms of his favourite red velvet chair and pressed his fingers together, a vaulted arc through which his voice fell slowly towards me from long ago.

Patrick and Eleanor went to a piano recital at the Contessa's villa. Eleanor made herself ready with wellington boots and goggles of mascara. They traipsed up the garden path, Eleanor sulking a little as Chopin sprinkled from an open window. In the music-room a young German, his pate bright bald, milked the Steinway. Eleanor ate macaroons and removed one wellington to scratch at her instep while the other hand hogged more biscuits. Five minutes into the recital she leaned over and whispered, 'Very soon you will have to excuse me. I am tone deaf to all instruments except the bagpipes.'

They left. Eleanor pocketed a last macaroon as she rose from her chair.

Patrick and Eleanor furnished themselves with two typewriters; Patrick's was strewn with papers, Eleanor's with roses, and they conceived their first baby. They returned to London as winter began and Gabriella Laura was born. Eleanor was entranced.

Patrick found a tiny flat in Islington and its one room was a talcum-powdered temple to the baby. Eleanor spent hours each day mooning by the cradle where Gabriella slept, watching her tiny hands unclench and float like seaweed against her shawl. In awe and incredulous at the baby's ability to survive, she leaned over the cradle night after night, prodding the child until an angry yell verified the miracle of existence. Patrick, thirty years older, had sired three children by the time he met Eleanor, but had never been given or taken the time to be with them. They were grown-up now, the same age as Eleanor, and he found himself enraptured by his new daughter, beguiled into family life.

Patrick found it impossible to write in the cramped flat and longed to take Eleanor and Gabriella back to the sun. He borrowed a house on the borders of France and Italy, and in the spring they drove off into the snowbound Apennines. Patrick loved driving. He wore leather gloves stippled with holes and glasses with green lenses. He had a navy-blue Mercedes with a bench front seat and a steering wheel as white as bone. In this car, which he and Eleanor christened Sadie Benz, they sped through tiny French villages, the baby's clean nappies streaming like wedding bunting from the windows as Eleanor attempted to dry them.

Spring came slowly, buds blurred on the misted trees where rooks wrenched off twigs and flapped away with them to build nests. I was eleven and I took an exam to see if I could win a scholarship to Mary Hall's Girls School.

Mummy drove me to the school one watery March morning. I wore my camel coat. I hated it. The sleeves were too short and the fabric smelt of damp and scratched at my neck. I felt hot and cross and restricted. The sky was grey and heavy as the tarmac on the road as we crept towards Norwich in the mini-van. I glanced into the back of the car and cringed with embarrassment at the piles of sweet wrappers and old newspapers. A spare tyre, its inner tube hanging out like a bloated intestine, was wedged behind my seat, old socks and forgotten hats strewn across its black bulk. Shame, and a deeper shame of my shame, flushed over me, and I prayed that no one at the school would see our car.

Mummy was callously oblivious to the mini-van's aesthetic faults, and indeed to her own, although she promised to take off her blonde wig as soon as we had driven through Aylthorpe. She had been stopped by the police a few weeks before for having

4

orange nylon string spewing from the engine of the car. The police asked to see her driving licence. She didn't have one. She stared blankly at the officers and was let off with a stern caution not to drive again. Jubilant at her escape, she came home and searched through a trunk full of hats until she found a stringy blonde wig brought to Mildney by someone in a transvestite phase. She wore it every time she went out and she looked like a madwoman. Her pale skin battled and lost with the brassy blonde tufts of the wig, and her own dark wiry hair puffed out from beneath it in a cloud. She completed the disguise with a pair of purple-tinted glasses left by another visitor and a big brown fur coat. Daddy saw her sallying forth and raised his eyes to heaven. 'Can this possibly be my wife? My love, you will be locked up if you are seen like that.'

This morning she wasn't wearing her dark glasses, but the wig was perched like a beret towards the back of her head and the fur coat was done up with nappy pins, their pastel pink and white heads protruding awkwardly from the thick brown pelt. 'I'll undo it when we get there,' she soothed, accelerating to pass a pedestrian.

I looked out at the road. A cyclist hissed past in the rain. 'Mummy, we're going very slowly.'

As the words left my mouth the van groaned, shuddered and died. Mummy and I looked at one another and burst into nervous tears. We pushed the car to the edge of the road and sat on the bonnet. I leaned over and pulled the wig from her head; neither of us spoke. A great green car pulled up and a bald man with long leather riding-boots and a moustache got out of it.

5

'Oh God.' Mummy stiffened beside me. 'Now we're going to be murdered as well.'

The man stood in front of us. He towered over the little mini-van.

'Where are you going?' His voice was far more gentle than his appearance.

'My daughter has an interview in Norwich at eleven o'clock,' said Mummy, 'and this bloody car has stopped.'

'I'll take you,' said the man. 'My name is John Leighton. I live in Melton.'

I wiped my nose on my sleeve – it was better than using the crisp packet which was all Mummy could find when I asked her for a handkerchief – and looked at his car. It was very shiny. The faint drizzle of rain, which on our mini-van had produced a viscous surface of slime, glistened in tiny clear bubbles along the green bonnet. We got in, sliding and squeaking across deep leather seats. The man drove us to Norwich not saying a word, chain-smoking long gold-tipped cigarettes. Mummy thanked him and he smiled and nodded his naked head before driving off into the shunting traffic.

'How extraordinary,' said Mummy. 'I think it bodes well for your interview, don't you?' I didn't answer. I couldn't speak because my tongue was glued to the roof of my mouth.

The school smelt of polish; bright clean floors vanished around corners. All the doors along the corridors were closed. Behind one I heard a chorus of voices chanting Latin while industrious silence welled from others. I imagined hundreds of girls concentrating very hard, and I felt isolated and insignificant. We sat outside the headmistress's office. I gazed vacantly at the neat white label; it said: 'Miss Floyd'. I looked at my hands and noticed that all my nails were tipped with dark crescents of grease from the car. I clenched my fists. The 'Miss Floyd' door opened and a rotund lady came out. She had thin, fine hair brushed carefully into a peak to minimize the pink glow of her scalp. A few flakes of skin had settled on her shoulders. She was very small. She smiled and shook hands with Mummy.

'Gabriella, will you please come with me,' she trilled. Mummy kissed me and whispered, 'Good luck, darling,' and I followed Miss Floyd into her office.

The room smelt of sweet coffee and Marie biscuits. My stomach rumbled loudly. Miss Floyd waved me to a chair and sat down behind a huge desk, empty except for a horribly blank sheet of paper. I felt less nervous when I noticed that only her head and shoulders rose above the desk, and I sat up very straight so that I was almost taller than she was. She asked me a few boring questions about my present school and what subjects I liked best. Then she said, 'And what are your hobbies?'

Mummy had prepared me for this question, and we had mapped out a charming, enthusiastic answer full of pony clubs, wild flowers and brass-rubbing. I was astonished to hear my voice, crystal clear and confident: 'I am interested in the dead. I go to all the churches near home on my bicycle and I look at every grave and try to imagine the lives of the people who are buried there. My favourites, although they are the saddest, are the young men who were killed in the First World War, and the whole families of tiny children who must have perished through scarlet fever.'

Miss Floyd's smile faded, her thin eyebrows rose into her thin hair and she fiddled with a pencil. Her confusion buoyed up my confidence; I told her everything Daddy had ever told me about history, and wildly ascribed these tales to people whose graves I said I had seen. By the time I reached the Gunpowder Plot (inventing a trip to London to see the Houses of Parliament) she had heard enough.

'You have a lively imagination.' Her voice dipped into a sour squawk and she disappeared behind her desk as she bobbed forwards to push her chair out. I craned my neck to see if she had to jump to reach the floor. 'And history is indeed fascinating. Come. Let us join your mother.'

Beaming victory, I followed her out of the office to Mummy. We said goodbye and left.

With every step away from the school my confidence ebbed. I thought of the sour squawk and the chilly comment about my imagination, and shrank. I told Mummy what I had said and she was horrified.

'What on earth possessed you? It isn't even remotely true, is it?'

I shook my head. 'It just seemed to be the right thing to say. I couldn't help it, it just all came out.'

'Never mind.' Mummy stopped to hug me. Daddy was waiting outside in the Mercedes. Mummy had rung him and asked him to collect us. He saw our tight faces as we walked to the car.

'I think we all deserve a treat now,' he said. Mortified, I sat like a statue as Mummy told him about the car's disgraceful behaviour.

I knew that Daddy and Mummy desperately wanted me to win a scholarship and that they couldn't afford to send me to a good school if I didn't get one. Longed-for virtue and my recent unexpected rebellion warred within me. I wanted another chance.

'Shall I write her a letter saying I made it all up?'

I hoped Mummy would say no. She did.

'What happened, my love?' Daddy asked, but I didn't answer because at that moment we were driving up a concrete ramp into a cavernous multi-storey car park. 'There is a delicious Chinese restaurant in here,' said Daddy.

'How on earth do you know?' Mummy was incredulous.

Daddy winked. 'The world is full of unsolved mysteries, my dear Eleanor.'

'I suppose you come here for indulgent little lunches when I take the children to the dentist.'

Daddy laughed. 'The mystery is solved.'

The restaurant walls were lined with glass tanks full of drifting tropical fish. Between the tanks, thick glass panes gave a misty view into the car park. Daddy chose a table where we could look out at the Mercedes. Mummy yelped. 'God. No wonder you like it here. Do we have to look at the car?'

'You may look the other way,' said Daddy, 'but I want to look at the car.'

I had never been to a restaurant with just Mummy and Daddy. I felt sophisticated. The boys will be jealous, I thought.

Daddy lit a cigarette. 'Was the school decent? Did you like it, my love? You shall not go there if you didn't.'

'I won't get the chance.' And I told him about my lies.

Daddy laughed. 'I see you have a brain underneath all that hair.'

'Are you angry?' I blurted out.

Mummy and Daddy answered together. 'No, of course we aren't.'

'You are a very clever girl,' said Daddy, 'and I can see no reason why you should have to go to school at all.'

Mummy glared at him, but he pretended not to see and ordered me a frozen orange with sorbet in the place of flesh.

O n Burns Night when Gabriella was one, a fat cherub with eyes like china saucers and dimpled knees, her brother Archibald Robert was born. Patrick and Eleanor had returned from Italy to their damp Islington basement. They were broke. Whenever it rained, thick white slugs slouched their way up the glass of the french windows. Gabriella was sent to stay with Eleanor's parents in Scotland; she learnt to walk, tottering gnomish in a red hooded suit, and she forgot her mother.

Eleanor went to Harrods and bought a bearskin hat for Patrick to take to the icy plains of Buffalo. He had been offered a post as writer in residence at the university, and the fee was too large to refuse. Eleanor waved him off at the airport and went into hospital to give birth to her son. She knew no one in London; her only visitor was the ghost of Graham Kingsley who had died a week or two before. She and Graham's spirit spent a merry afternoon recalling evenings wet with whisky and tears in the pubs of Soho, and then Eleanor and her baby caught the train to Scotland.

At Aberdeen her daughter, arms stretched out behind for

balance, taxied down the platform towards her. Tearful, Eleanor ran to Gabriella and knelt to embrace her. Gabriella screamed as this tall woman bore down on her, terrifying and unidentifiable in a cavernous cloak. Her grandmother, a tiny smile playing on her lips, stepped forward and picked Gabriella up. 'It's all right, darling. This is Mummy. You remember Mummy, don't you? She's brought you a baby brother.'

Gabriella squatted in front of the moses basket and patted the baby's soft head. 'Brodie,' she said, beaming round at her mother and grandmother standing behind her, tensed for her reaction.

Archibald Robert lay festooned in Cameron lace on the spindly sofa in his grandparents' drawing-room. Gabriella had stumbled through her first two words (Va Va, her name for herself, and Boys, the other people she was interested in) when she met her brother. Eleanor tried to call her Gabriella, but she shook her head and would not answer. She was Va Va now, and her baby was Brodie. He was small and pink and crumpled; Va Va was delighted by his inability to do any of the things at which she excelled, like walking and talking, and she adored him because he was hers, everyone told her so. She looked upon him as something to care for, keenly embracing the role of Big Sister. He incurred her displeasure, though, when he learned to walk. As he forged his first moon-man steps towards the doorway of a room where Eleanor sat, fury welled in Va Va at her mother's words of encouragement. Indignation pricked her skin like sunburn and, gathering all her crosspatch feelings, she rushed to slam the door, separating Brodie and his success from Eleanor's proud smiling eyes.

Eleanor had left Scotland in a tangled trail of purple silk, fishnet stockings and high-heeled shoes. She was seventeen. She went to Oxford and fell asleep in her finals. A local newspaper printed a picture of her slumbering under the headline 'A Sleeping Beauty'. Lurking with a hangover in Blackwell's bookshop, she picked up a volume of poetry by Patrick Lincoln; it froze her spine and she fell in love. She moved to London and took a job as a waitress in Lyons Corner House, and then another, folding scarves in Liberty's. It was 1962 and she had never seen anyone rock and roll and had only watched television once, when her father had borrowed a set to see the Queen's coronation. In her dreary bedsit Eleanor made tea by heating water on an iron. She did not know how to boil an egg or slice a loaf of bread; she became very thin and returned to Scotland for a while with a beehive hair-do and a lot of fanciful notions about poets.

T wo weeks after the interview, Mummy received a letter from Mary Hall's Girls School confirming my place for the autumn term. She was thrilled and so was I until a terrible thought occurred to me.

'Will I have to go on Saturdays? I can't. What about riding?'

Daddy was reading the paper at the kitchen table with two-year-old Poppy sitting on his knee. He looked up, raising his spectacles on to his forehead. 'No one goes to school on Saturdays,' he said. 'No one works on Saturdays either.'

Dan appeared from the playroom. 'It's Saturday now. It's sweetie day. When are we going to the shop to get our sweets? I can take Poppy on my own now.'

'No you can't.' Mummy heaved the iron door-stop back to its position against the fridge door where it squatted as a sentry against the fiendish cunning of the cats. 'Four simply isn't old enough to cross the road. Brodie can take you.'

'I'll have to go to school on Saturdays.' Brodie was invisible, perched behind the sheets which hung low over the Aga to dry. 'When I go to King Henry's I'll have to wear shorts and go on Saturdays.' Brodie had also just passed his scholarship

14

exam and, with relentless dolour, was not looking forward to his new school.

Daddy folded the newspaper. 'I'm going for a drive to the coast. I may have fish and chips for lunch . . .' and he let his sentence trail as children engulfed him, baying to be included.

It took hours putting on coats, and in the middle Flook returned from his dig in the garden. Flook was nine and had for a year been engrossed in a project he started at school to discover the history of Mildney. He was breathless with excitement. 'Look what I've found. I think it's prehistoric.' He held up a skull the size of his own head.

'It's a goat,' said Dan immediately, and Flook sighed. 'Of course it's a goat, but it might be a prehistoric goat, or from Roman times.'

Daddy held the skull up to the light. 'We shall start our museum with this,' he said. 'Flook, you have the bones of a great archaeologist; now let's get the hell out of here and go to Cromer.'

Daddy was never late and he hated dawdling. Mummy found it impossible to leave the house on time, and whenever they went out together Daddy would sit in the car for twenty minutes revving the engine and shouting, while Mummy rushed through the house muttering 'I'm coming, you silly sod' under her breath.

We waited for her in the car. Brodie and I slid along the shiny leather of the front seat to make room for Flook. Mummy came out of the house without a coat. 'I'll stay here. All those people are coming this evening and I've got so much to do. Have a lovely time, darlings.'

We bumped down the drive, Dan and Poppy kneeling up to look out of the back window. 'Dobe's coming too,' said Dan, as we accelerated out of the village. Our anarchic Dobermann had a private mission to outpace the car, and he always tried to come too. He hurtled past the Mercedes as Daddy slowed down and, saliva foaming at his jaws, stood triumphant in the middle of the road.

'For Christ's sake,' sighed Daddy, and opened a door. Dobe scrambled in, licking faces politely, and positioned himself with his head resting on Daddy's shoulder to help him navigate.

We had fish and chips, then filed into Daddy's favourite junk shop. 'It's Liza's birthday today. We must find something to give her this evening. Poppy shall choose it,' said Daddy. Liza had once been Daddy's wife, before he knew Mummy, and their three children, Dominic, Helen and Theresa, were all grown-up. They called Daddy 'Patrick' and they didn't feel like siblings to us; they were as old as Mummy and had children of our age.

Liza came often to Mildney, driving perilously on her orange moped and clad in a coordinating cagoule. She always brought a bottle of gin, telling us, 'This is mother's ruin, and your mother and I are longing to be ruined.' She was funny and kind, we liked the way she danced in the Drinking Room and teased Daddy. He called her 'darling heart' and said, 'Come and tell me some lies, dear Liza.'

Poppy chose a teapot in the shape of a Christmas pudding. Daddy was impressed. 'My love, you have exquisite taste,' he said to his tiny daughter, and we left the shop, pausing to purchase a rusty colander for Mummy.

Brodie, Flook and I got out of the car on our drive. The boys vanished to go fishing and I plodded through the dusk to feed my pony Shalimar. Yanking tufts of hay from the bulging bale, I was inspired. 'If there is Saturday school, I won't tell Mummy.' Pleased with this plan, I shuffled down to Shalimar's field with a wedge of dusty hay.

Liza arrived at tea-time, her face glowing pink from her forty-mile moped ride. She hugged Mummy. 'Eleanor, this is a treat. I'm sure I'm too old for a tea-party, I think I'm sixty-one, but I can't quite remember.'

Taking off her crash helmet she dragged her fingers through her dark blonde hair and lit a cigarette. Liza looked ageless. She had deep cracks round her mouth and eyes from laughing, but they almost vanished when she was happy, and she usually seemed happy. She loved coming to Mildney because she lived alone. 'I'm thirsty for conversation. Tell me a joke,' she begged Dan, but he shook his head. 'I'm eating cake,' he mumbled. Brodie and Flook were still fishing, so she sat down with me and fumbled in her pocket for a letter. 'It's from Helen and the girls. Do you remember Zoe and Vinnie, my granddaughters?'

I nodded. 'Of course she does,' said Daddy. 'They are her nieces, in a manner of speaking.'

'Half-nieces actually,' I replied, and Liza laughed.

'I suppose they are; Helen is your half-sister, after all. How nice to have a family to extend at will.'

Brodie and Flook appeared. 'Dominic's here,' said Brodie. 'He's brought a box of drink.'

'Is this a family reunion?' Liza raised her eyebrows and Mummy laughed.

'No. Only Dominic, he wanted to surprise you on your birthday.'

Liza and Daddy went through to the Drinking Room and Flook and I rolled our eyes. 'I suppose they have to celebrate Liza's birthday,' said Flook, 'but I wish they didn't have to get drunk to do it.'

Mummy frowned at him. 'Don't be mean. Liza loves parties, and she wanted to be here with all of us for her birthday. Dominic has simply come to see his mother, and a few other people will be here after you've gone to bed, so try and be pleasant, please.'

Brodie, Flook and I glared back at her. 'You know we hate Drinking Evenings,' I muttered, but Mummy didn't hear me; she was helping Poppy down from the table where she sat marooned among the debris of tea.

Patrick wrote his first poem when he was nine. As a small boy he read precociously and widely. He spent his lunch money on poems and, inspired, wrote his own with great delight. When he was eighteen he sent a poem to David Archer, a publisher with a tiny bookshop in Parton Street. Archer invited him to tea. Nervously entering the chaotic, crammed shop, Patrick saw before him a pale young man swaying high upon a stepladder. 'Be an angel, hand me that hammer,' said Archer and Patrick did so. Archer brought out Patrick's first volume of poetry and introduced him to T.S. Eliot. Eliot asked Patrick to send some poems to him at Faber, and a few days later a letter arrived confirming that Patrick was to be published by them. At twenty, Patrick had leapt over the straight blue line which in those days took young men from public school to Oxford and then into publishing and being published. He became famous.

Like Eleanor but twenty years earlier, Liza found Patrick's poems in a bookshop, read them and fell in love. She wrote to him, offering money and an escape from Japan, where he was teaching at a university when war broke out. He accepted and sailed across the Pacific to California where Liza met him.

They began a love affair which was to span almost two decades and produce Dominic, Helen and Theresa.

Patrick and Liza rarely lived together, and never married. During a lull in their relationship Patrick met an *ingénue* called Nancy with a fleece of blonde hair and round blue eyes like baubles on a Christmas tree. They got married and left London for a cottage in Sussex where the roses were overblown and the tap spewed sand as well as water. Nancy wanted to write, but she wanted to have babies more. Patrick forbade her to become pregnant. Nancy defied him. He drank a bottle of whisky to fortify himself, then forced her to sit in a scalding bath while he poured gin down her protesting throat. She was young and scared and she forgave him. He tortured her, a maniacal curiosity roused in him to see how much she would take.

One morning he called her into the garden. Sacrificial in her white nightdress, Nancy stood in the orchard against a bowed apple tree. Patrick picked up an apple from the grass and placed it on her head. He took a bow and arrow and, assuring her that he had been practising, shot the apple through the core. She could take no more. Days later Nancy ran away into the arms of Patrick's best friend, and they disappeared. Raging and bereft, Patrick left the house in pursuit of her. He didn't shut the front door or turn off the wireless. He went and never came back. He drove up and down England searching for Nancy but no one dared tell him where or with whom she had gone. In desperation he went to see her mother in Harlow. She tried to shut the door in his face, but he forced his way into her kitchen. Seeing his grief and his determination, Nancy's mother relented a little and made him a cup of tea.

'Where is Nancy?'

'I cannot tell you. I will never tell you.'

Patrick glowered and lit a cigarette. He looked up at the glinting litter of china and silver candlesticks on the mantelpiece. Propped against a small mauve shepherdess was an envelope. Patrick was sitting at the far end of the room but he could make out the familiar shape of Nancy's name. Her mother made tea and talked stiltedly of the route back to London and the weather. Patrick answered, his eyes fixed on the envelope, straining to read the address. Nancy's mother saw the direction of his gaze and continued to talk. Patrick left. He never found Nancy.

Patrick returned to Liza, but the affair dwindled and by the time he met Eleanor it had been reduced to an uneasy friendship. Liza sustained cool hostilities during Eleanor's pregnancy, but when Va Va was born, unbent a little.

In the years that followed, the tangled relationship between Liza, Eleanor and Patrick unravelled and the two women became close friends, excluding Patrick from their long late-night conversations. 'I could never live with him, not even when the children were small. I don't know how you can remain sane,' Liza said to Eleanor time and time again. When Patrick dragged her from parties by her arm, her collar, her hair, and threw wine over men she spoke to, Eleanor vowed she would leave him for ever. But she stayed.

E very moment that I was not at school or asleep I spent with Shalimar. He had come on my ninth birthday, a black furry creature, roses latched by their thorns to his thick mane. His ears pricked up when he first saw me and his eyes gleamed with what I took to be love but which turned out to be malevolence. My own pony. For two years I was content. I rode across stubble fields and through woods. I schooled him over my home-made jumps and pampered him with hoof manicures, shampoos and hour-long grooming sessions until his barrel-shaped body gleamed. But Shalimar was too small to contain my sprawling equine obsession, and when I had performed every possible stunt on him, including swimming him across the mill pond and riding home facing backwards, I wanted more.

Mummy took me to meet a friend of hers who had a stable full of racehorses and hunters. Sophy Lane agreed that I should come and help muck out each weekend in exchange for rides on these peerless steeds. Sophy was the zenith of horsy glamour. She wore a headscarf knotted at the nape of her neck and she walked with a swagger. Her eyelids were sapphire-tinted, her lips a swoop of pearly pink. I longed to look like her but lacked the courage to affect a headscarf or make-up except in the privacy of my bedroom. Sophy's husband Boots was a thin dark man, curved like a riding crop. He strutted through the stables in his yellow cowboy chaps, making sleazy jokes and smoking untipped cigarettes one after another after another.

The stables were at Sophy's parents' house, a dour greystone mansion with ranks of windows hooded by pale shutters. Sophy's mother, Lady Warton, short, stout, with white hair and a pointed voice, came riding every day decked in spotless jodhpurs and a perfectly tied cravat.

Their ordered lives, the horses' ordered lives, the regular hours and the strict routine dazzled me. At the stables I mucked out five looseboxes in a row and thought of home, wondering why we couldn't keep our rooms tidy or even make our beds each day. Mummy patiently listened as I poured out every detail of my passion, but when I tried to tell Daddy he said, 'I have never found the conversation of horses even mildly entertaining. You are like your Mummy, you speak their language.' I was sorry not to be able to discuss my dressage test with him, but at least Mummy was interested.

Daddy shuddered and slunk out of the kitchen when we started talking about horses. He unwrapped blue tissue paper from bottles of wine and went into the Drinking Room. Mummy bit her lip and sighed.

Much later, in the middle of the night, I woke up. The landing shook as someone lurched against the banisters. 'You fucking bitch. Get out of this house now. Do you hear me?'

A throbbing scream echoed along the corridors. I knew it

was Mummy; I wanted to help her but my limbs had turned to dough. Glass shattered in the hall, I thought of the animals' soft paws and winced. Mummy tiptoed into my room.

'Are you all right?' She sat on my bed; touching her face I felt tears warm on her cheeks and I hated Daddy. 'Where's he gone?'

Mummy laughed shakily. 'To get his gun, but I've hidden it.'

I clutched at her arm, fear holding my breath. 'Why does he do this? Why does he want to shoot you?'

'He's mad when he's drunk.' Mummy wiped her eyes on the sheets. 'He doesn't mean it, but a demon takes over when he drinks.'

Suddenly he was in the room. 'Eleanor, get out of that child's bed and find me my goddam gun.'

I burst into tears. 'Go away, Daddy, don't be horrible to Mummy.'

'For Christ's sake go to bed, Patrick,' Mummy begged. 'You'll wake all the children.'

He came nearer, I became frantic. 'Go away, go away, I hate you.'

Daddy backed off, cursing. Mummy and I heard his footsteps retreating and his bedroom door slam. Mummy sighed, 'Thank God. He's gone to bed. I'm going to take Poppy up to Louise's house tonight. I'll be back in the morning.'

Louise was calm and made strong tea. I wanted to go too, to sleep in Louise's safe house at the other end of the village. 'Can I come?'

'Darling, don't worry. You know he would never hurt any of

24

you. He loves you. He loves me too, but I'm not spending the night dodging his drunken fury.'

Mummy and Poppy were back for breakfast, but the next Sunday morning Mummy wasn't there. Poppy was.

'Where's Mummy?' Their bedroom smelt metallic and stuffy when I opened the door, and Daddy lay groaning beneath a heap of tumbled blankets.

'What time is it? Seven. Jesus Christ. She's in hospital.'

Nausea clawed me and I marched up to the bed and leaned over. 'Why is she in hospital, Daddy?'

He covered his face with his hands. 'She fell down the stairs. An ambulance came and took her to hospital. Now get off my back.'

He's guilty. Very guilty, I thought, and phoned Louise, straining to keep calm.

'Your Mum's fine,' she said. 'She got a black eye falling down the stairs and we sent her to hospital in case her nose was broken. She'll be back today.'

I knew she hadn't fallen down the stairs, and I wanted Daddy to know that I knew. So I refused to make him a cup of tea or any breakfast. He had a front tooth missing and a swollen face. It served him right. We drove to the hospital to collect Mummy.

'Are we having another baby?' asked Dan on the way.

'No we are not,' said Daddy.

Flook kicked Daddy's seat as we drove. 'You shouldn't fight with Mummy. You'll be sorry, you know.'

'I already am.'

Daddy did look very sorry, but I wanted to be sure. 'You'll

be lucky if Mummy forgives you,' I said coldly. 'You should give up drinking. It's gross and it makes you gross.'

I had gone too far. Daddy slammed his foot on the accelerator. 'Oh shut up, you lot. I've got a headache.'

The shouting and fighting stopped soon afterwards, and I was convinced that we had changed Daddy's nature with our evangelical enthusiasm for making him sorry.

Brodie and Va Va spent their first summer together sitting in large saucepans of water in the cratered bomb site which was their Islington garden. Inside the flat, beneath the stone gaze of a golden seraph and an Egyptian king, Patrick wrote while Eleanor, unaware of the existence of shops beyond Harrods, tried to keep her children fed and clothed on an income which didn't come in.

Patrick gave her some money and offered to look after the children while she went and bought herself something to wear. Eleanor went shopping, the prospect of a new dress eclipsing the suspicion she should have felt at Patrick's uncharacteristic behaviour. At lunch-time she returned. She hugged the babies; they were both dressed in velvet. She turned to Patrick, astonished that he should have dressed them at all. He stood by the tiled fireplace, an expression of benign surreptitiousness on his face.

'Thomas Bevin and Trixie will be here in half an hour,' he said. 'We are going to baptize the children.'

Eleanor railed at his trickery, gathering Brodie and Va Va on to her knee like a New Testament mother faced with King

Herod. 'It's not that I don't want them to be Catholic. But I don't like your methods.'

Patrick was meek. 'How right you are, my love, how right you are.'

The doorbell rang. Thomas Bevin, a Jesuit priest with a brow furrowed like celery, arrived with Trixie, a friend of Eleanor's from Oxford. Bevin was to officiate. Trixie was to be godmother and Patrick had selected a young poet, Raj Singh, as godfather. He had failed to get hold of any other Catholics, so had decided that the children should share godparents.

Bevin sat in a crumbling armchair covered in mattress ticking. He sipped a glass of wine and ignored the half-eaten chocolate biscuit Va Va placed on his knee.

'Raj is not a suitable person to bear responsibility for any child's soul,' he announced. 'You will have to find another godfather, Patrick.'

Half an hour remained before the service. Patrick and Eleanor resigned themselves to picking someone off the street. They were joking about how to spot a Catholic in Islington when the doorbell rang again.

Kevin Toller, a lazy journalist with a taste for whisky, slouched in fondling a bottle of Famous Grouse. 'Patrick,' he said, puffing whisky fumes into the little room, 'I came to share this with you and to watch the Cup Final.'

'Dear boy,' said Patrick, 'you are here by divine intervention. We are baptizing my children and you shall be their godfather.'

Toller protested, to no avail. Va Va and Brodie were christened in black and green velvet and Eleanor's parents were very angry.

*   *   *

Patrick's first love was the Muse and she danced in the aisles of the Church of Rome. He talked about her as if she were a difficult girlfriend. 'She's bitched me up again,' he growled after a day of crumpling paper into balls and raining them down around the rubbish bin. He abided by none of the conventions which make a good Catholic, but he believed in the saints and suffered from guilt.

His faith was handed down to him by his mother, an Irish peasant whose only education was the poetry she had learnt by heart at school. She was a fervent Catholic, and worshipped with an ardour perfectly pitched between the Brompton Oratory and the Queen's Elm pub in Chelsea. Patrick's learning came not from school but from conversations with young monks at the Oratory who appeared like hungry starlings at his mother's table.

By the time Va Va was three, the basement flat in Islington could no longer contain the family. Eleanor was pregnant and Patrick was being driven insane by trying to write in a tiny room invaded by beaming, screaming children. They had no money with which to buy a house, and in desperation Patrick answered an advertisement in *The Times* for a house to rent in Norfolk. He drove up to see it and was enchanted.

The front door was open when they arrived at Mildney, a house Eleanor was seeing for the first time. Furious on the flagstones of the hall, spiky like an unopened chestnut, was a tiny ginger kitten. Out of the Mercedes slithered Marmalade the black cat, spitting vicious urban expletives at the kitten before slinking into the shadows of the house.

Tired and hot, with legs patched pink where they had stuck to the leather seats of the car, Va Va and Brodie got out and looked at their new home. Mildney. A seventeenth-century farmhouse, part brick, part dimpled flint, and all damp. Va Va scarcely glanced at the house but looked across at the garden stretching away in every direction through tangles of flowers and crouched bushes. Under her feet an expanse of green loomed, as big as any in a London park. Her legs took over and, racing, she carved a circle in the long grass. Brodie followed, fingers splayed like feathers as they swooped faster and faster. Va Va somersaulted and fell on the grass. 'Listen. There's no noise, no noise at all.'

Brodie stood a moment and smiled. 'There is noise. I can hear the trees talking.'

They laughed, sinking, rolling like beached fish.

Patrick came out of the house and took their hands. 'Come, dear hearts, I have something to show you.' He led them round the beech hedge, which flamed high and gold above the lawn, and through a line of knobbly oaks. 'Close your eyes now,' he said, and the ground slid as he led them down a hill, fronds of bracken tickling their legs. Patrick stopped. 'Now look.'

They were on the bank of a slow, silent river; floating like blobs of ice-cream on the black surface were two swans.

'Look, Daddy, look! Swans. Can we keep them? What are their names? Where's that one's head?' The children's voices tumbled out, shrill and urgent. One swan, delving deep in the weeds beneath, uncoiled her long neck, rearing from the water.

She hissed menace and warning. Patrick led the children back up the bank.

'Those are Isabella and Isabeau,' he said. 'They are magical birds and at bedtime I will tell you their story.'

That night they sat together in bed, shoulders stiff with anticipation. Patrick began. Isabella and Isabeau were the guardians to the gates of Halicarnassus, the pillared home of Shalimar the winged horse. Brodie and Va Va, one moment barbed excitement, the next slumped, were asleep.

One spring afternoon Sophy took me out into the park by the lake. I was riding a new horse. His name was Nimrod and his Arab nostrils flared red excitement; he capered and swished his streaming auburn tail. Nimrod rolled the whites of his eyes. He quivered, then grabbed the bit and bolted. I clung on, exhilarated, as we floated over a gate and sped off through a grove of walnut trees. I tried to stop, afraid that he might slip, but I was too late. A branch slapped me in the face, cracking between my teeth, and I was swept to the ground.

I came round in hospital, stirred into consciousness by a fracas at my feet. A cluster of nurses twittered like sparrows. They had a knife. They wanted to cut off my boots. Mummy did not want them to. Her protective instincts were sharpened by the sight of my football-sized face and her inability to help me in any other way. I had broken my jaw. I lay on the stretcher, tears tightening the parts of my face I could still feel. I couldn't speak, nor could my numbed tongue feel any teeth in my mouth. A nurse noticed my distress and, interpreting it as grief for my riding boots, called off the battle.

Two operations later someone gave me a mirror. I had black

eyes, a stitched gash beneath my lip where my teeth had gone through and wire binding my mouth. Behind the wire my teeth were still there, yellow with blood and old saliva. Where my skin was not black with bruising it was greenish white and my face was pear-shaped. I stared in horror. 'This is not me. This is someone else. I am at home with Mummy and Daddy and the boys and Poppy.'

I pushed the mirror away and refused to look in one again until I left hospital three weeks later.

Daddy came to see me, his eyes full of tears. 'These bloody horses. It breaks my heart to see what they've done to you.' He smiled, shaking his head. 'My love, you are brave and foolish. I wish to God you wouldn't do it.'

Mummy kicked his ankle. He had promised not to mention his campaign to make me give up riding. Only my lips moved when I spoke. 'It wasn't the horse's fault. It was an accident.' I fell back against the pillow, sweat breaking with the effort of utterance.

Daddy kissed my forehead. 'You have courage. I am proud of you. I wish you could come home with us today.' He moved back to let Brodie talk to me.

Brodie had been hysterical since my accident. He refused to believe I was alive until he saw me himself. His eyes flickered over my warped face. He burst into tears and whispered to Mummy. She took him out and came back moments later, alone. 'Brodie's been sick,' she said calmly. 'He's very shocked, I must take him home.'

It was lonely and tedious in hospital. I could not eat, so even the small diversion of mealtimes was denied me. For protein

I was given mugs of yeasty Complan which I sipped gingerly, revolted by the potent iron taste and thick blood-warmth of the drink. Mummy's and Daddy's visits were my daily high-point, but through the long dull afternoons I was vulnerable, supine. Friends of my parents, people I hardly knew and people I didn't like at all visited me. I lay in my bed, gloom mounting, as these well-meaning folk ambled down the ward looking for me. My face was too sore to bury in the pillows or duck beneath the blankets. I had no choice but to sit there waiting, lips stretched back over my steel-filled mouth in a permanent, unwanted grin.

Reverend Thompson, who had come to our primary school to tell us the facts of life, brought a box of Turkish Delight. I hated Turkish Delight. Two of the old ladies from the village made a special trip on the OAPs' bus. They had sacrificed their bingo for me and I was not pleased. They were part of the coven of busybodies at the bottom of our drive. They loathed Dobe because he once went down to the village wearing some red lacy camiknickers we had dressed him in. I knew they were only visiting me out of nosiness. I frowned throughout their stay as they tittered and gibed about the village fete and the vicar winning a bottle of gin. All the visitors sat at the end of my bed and gazed at me with eager pity. I glared back, mute and frustrated in my mouth harness, furiously embarrassed by the long silences which persisted through all visits save those of my family.

Sophy came, bringing her two-year-old son, Adam. Adam thought he was a dog. He had spent his whole small life in the stables with dogs or in the car with dogs and he didn't speak, he barked. He sat on my feet whimpering and then uttered a soft yap and smiled. Mummy arrived, absently patting him as she reached to kiss me. 'Good boy, Adam, good boy.' She got out a paper bag and handed it to me.

'Darling, I brought you these. I chose lots of different kinds for you from Mr Cardew's. He sends his love.' She beamed encouragement. In the bag a dense mass of wrapped toffees rustled in their pretty floral papers. There were red ones and green ones, purple ones with pink flowers and yellow and blue ones. Dozens of them. All flaunting their chewiness. All mocking my affliction. I looked at Mummy, eyes stark at her stupidity; grunts of horror gurgled in my throat. She looked back at me and recognition of her wrong dawned. She started to laugh. Her eyes creased up and disappeared; tears eased down her cheeks as she continued to laugh. Embarrassed, Sophy left. I chucked a few toffees to Adam. He picked them up in his mouth and trotted after his mother. Mummy still laughed. Finally I did too, wincing as mirth tore through the wires in my gums. Mummy stayed a long time and when she left, I noticed that she had eaten all the toffees.

When I returned home from hospital Dobe wasn't there. 'Where is he?' I still spoke through clenched teeth like a Dalek; the wires were not being removed for six weeks. Mummy sat down and pulled me towards her.

'Darling, I have something very sad to tell you.' My stomach churned and I began to cry, knowing already that Dobe was dead. 'Dobe had a heart attack just there, over by the sink, last Tuesday. He jumped up to steal some food, then crashed to the floor. He didn't suffer. He was so well and happy and then he was dead – no pain or fear.'

I shook as I cried, wanting to bawl like a baby, prevented by my caged jaws.

'Why didn't you tell me?' I sobbed, but I knew Mummy was right when she said, 'It would have been awful for you to have known and not to have been here.'

She took me out to the Wilderness where Daddy and the boys had buried Dobe. I lay in the grass and wept until I was empty. I felt robbed and cheated. I hadn't been there. I hadn't dug his grave or said goodbye. I hadn't known and he would never be back.

Eleanor's stomach was huge and hot like an oven when Va Va hugged her. She was going to have a baby. She needed to rest, Patrick said, but she never seemed to lie down. She was always in some room Va Va had not noticed before, hanging up curtains, sneezing as she dusted the mantelpiece.

Too young for school, Brodie and Va Va stayed outside exploring their domain. They lay flat on the lawn gazing up at the limitless sky. It throbbed high above and they watched, trying never to blink as tiny birds flew up and up, faint dots on pale paper vanishing into a cloud.

Rory Francis was born before Va Va and Brodie had conquered the whole garden. They hardly noticed his advent. They had discovered a series of tiny streams in murky scrubland and had hunted out a moss-green crocodile, his jaws wide and gnarled. They planned to tame him and put him in the barns.

The new baby, sweetly scented and interestingly soft when poked, was nice enough, but not as exciting as the crocodile. Also he was not a girl. Va Va pretended he was. 'She's a little girl actually,' she crisply informed visitors.

Eleanor left Va Va and Brodie to their own devices; she made a holster out of an Indian scarf, tied the baby over her shoulder and continued to put the house straight. To swaddle Rory from black November skies she sang to him, a song about sailing down the Nile in a felucca. He became Flook and was never called Rory again.

In February Eleanor sent Patrick to meet a train. Out of the guard's van emerged his birthday present. A puppy. A Dobermann puppy who had travelled from Cornwall curled up in a washing-basket. Eleanor had found him in *Exchange & Mart* and saved up her family allowance, increased by the advent of Flook, to purchase him. Patrick's imagination failed him. 'He must be called Dobe,' he said. 'There is no other name for this remarkable hound.' He was enormously proud of Dobe's pedigree, and hung the certificate on the wall in the garage so that he could admire it while mending his car.

Patrick did not believe in discipline for dogs or children, and Dobe agreed. A sleek lunatic in black and tan, he lolled his tongue insolently when chastised. He never learnt to sit or stay, or to walk at heel. He roamed the fields and lanes for miles around Mildney, returning home to slump, groaning, into Patrick's favourite armchair. Patrick exercised him by driving the Mercedes round a three-mile block while Dobe ran beside the front wheel.

Eleanor climbed the stairs, Flook under one arm, a pile of clean washing cradled in the other. A thunderbolt of puppy hit her half-way up. It was Dobe in pursuit of a cat. She groped for the banister, and let go one of the soft white bundles to prevent herself from toppling. Va Va watched as the mound bounced slowly down the stairs. Outraged wails from the stone floor revealed that Flook was alive.

'Oh Christ. I thought it was the clothes.' Eleanor's voice was sharp with anguish. Flook, red and wriggling on the flagstones, was fine; his tightly bound shawl had given him a safe landing. Va Va stroked his head and looked at Eleanor, tears starting in her eyes when she saw them in her mother's.

B rodie's eleventh birthday hardly dawned at all. Iron-grey clouds yawned upwards for an hour, then slumped low over the fields. Brodie opened his presents, silent and withdrawn as he always was at times of expectation. Mummy was nervous about the things she had given him.

'He said he wanted uniforms so I've got two, one from the Second World War, one from the Crimea. Do you think he'll like them? He never likes anything I give him.'

'They sound fine,' I whispered because Brodie was in the kitchen, reading in the rocking-chair beneath a pile of purring cats. 'I've got him a fur hunter's hat from one of Daddy's junk shops. Daddy has got him a watch.'

Brodie unwrapped his parcels slowly. He said nothing. The rest of us chorused interest, trying to drown his silence. Mummy bit her lip, Daddy rolled his eyes, Brodie jumped up and left the room, presents cascading from his chair. Mummy found him crying in the playroom.

'What is it, darling? Don't you like your things? You can change them.'

Brodie sniffed. 'I do like some of them. I'm sorry.'

Mummy laughed, relieved that nothing more sinister lay in his tears. 'I'm used to none of you liking things. We'll go together and change them for the right ones.'

Brodie cheered up. Moments later he was laughing as he cut the cake Mummy had made. It was black, in the shape of an army helmet.

'Thank God he likes something,' Mummy whispered to Daddy.

Brodie grew tall in spurts. Some bits of him were small and childlike; others, his arms and legs, his mouth, his hands, strained large and adult in a schoolboy frame.

Flook was even bonier, translucent skin stretched over long legs which he whirled about on, dizzying himself, spinning, excited; quick to burst out laughing or roar in rage. Flook loved all his birthday presents and kept his things carefully in his tidy bedroom where his possessions were ranked in labelled drawers. Brodie's room was a cave where he huddled in bed reading, not noticing mould growing out of a forgotten cup of cocoa.

Daddy was finishing a book of verse. He never called his work poems and he referred to poetry as 'paltry' or 'poultry'. This confused journalists who came to interview him but he didn't care. He loathed being interviewed, but was powerless to prevent it. He refused to answer the telephone or to speak on it, so Mummy bore the brunt of requests to see him. Unable to think of any decent excuses, she always said, 'Yes, why not come on Saturday evening?'

Having just received a telephone call from the local paper, she sent me upstairs to tell Daddy who was coming. I knocked on the door of the study and found him at his desk, tapping with two fingers on the keys of his ancient typewriter. Beside him his notebooks teetered in a crooked column, the top one open at eye level.

'Space is the secret of writing verse,' he said. 'Space between the lines and the positioning of the words on the page.'

I told him about the local paper. 'I will see no one during the week. This is why I live in Norfolk. If I wanted to see people in the week, I would live on Piccadilly Circus,' he said.

'It's all right,' I soothed, 'they're coming on Saturday evening.'

'Good. In that case they can talk to someone else while I have a drink. I dare say there will be others here; that is what Saturday evening is for.'

I sighed. Saturday evenings meant a lot of people who never appeared on any other occasion, and a lot of drinking. I did not approve of drinking.

'Have you nearly finished today?' It was four o'clock, and Daddy usually came down when we returned from school. He worked in his study every morning until Poppy clambered up the stairs to call him down to have lunch with her and Dan, who had started morning school. Mummy never had any lunch; she said it made her fat and sleepy. 'You're as thin as trousers,' objected Poppy, and Daddy agreed. 'Your vanity will kill you,' he said, and Mummy frowned. 'Of course it won't. It's only lunch.'

When Daddy came down at tea-time, he and Brodie and Flook gathered wood for the fire. Mummy and Daddy had supper with us all and then Dan and Poppy went to bed. Daddy liked helping us with our homework, although his answers often bewildered our primary school teachers.

'I don't think Adolf Hitler did invent a car,' said Miss Coles cautiously, but Brodie was adamant. 'Actually he did. He invented the VW Beetle. Daddy says you can look it up if you don't believe him.' Miss Coles snapped her ginger brows together and changed the subject.

Eleanor gardened in the short skirts and high heels she had worn in London. She bought a grey mini-van at the auction; she had never passed her driving test, but she drove herself and the children, her hand a claw over the gear lever. She travelled slowly, jaws clenched in concentration, unable to speak for fear of crashing or breaking down.

She was lonely. At playgroup none of the other mothers looked like her when she swept in dangling an armful of children, a female cavalier in her big felt hat and balding fur coats, annual birthday presents, bought in junk shops by Patrick. She feared her brain was suffocating beneath a mound of children's toys and books, so she began to teach Va Va and Brodie ancient Greek. They sat at the kitchen table, wondering if this was what school was going to be like, while Eleanor recited tiny passages of Homer and chose words for them to learn. Flook sat in his high chair and beat his spoon in time when Va Va and Brodie chanted the alphabet: 'Alpha, beta, gamma, delta . . .'

Va Va, Brodie and Flook waited for Eleanor in the mini-van. They were going to be late for school. Dobe cavorted out of the house and bounced towards the beckoning fields. Va Va dragged her brothers out of the car and followed Dobe's erratic jumping-bean progress into the distance, certain that some great, incomprehensible excitement lurked beyond the next hill.

Crawling over a bank, Va Va straightened to help her brothers. Kip the gamekeeper, face set in fury like a jungle warrior's mask, materialized from the bracken. His gun towered, menacing, and the children shrank back, small before his great wrath. Flook howled and the others took his hands, Kip's fury pouring molten fear over them. Suddenly Dobe was there, icicle fangs bared to the gamekeeper. Kip lowered his gun and stomped back into the bracken.

Kip would have been a lot less frightened of Dobe if he had ever seen him hunting. Gangling and uncoordinated, Dobe vacuumed his way through hedges, muzzle glued to the ground, while his stubby tail waggled excitement above the scrub. The only time he caught anything was the day a confused and terrified rabbit ran headlong towards him and dropped dead at his feet.

Dobe was better with aeroplanes. His mornings were spent leaping across the back field like a kangaroo as he tried to grab low-flying jets out of the sky. He never exactly caught one, but his menacing seemed to have an effect. Twice Eleanor saw planes fall from the clouds to crash in the water-meadows.

Washing baby clothes in the kitchen sink, she looked out of the window. A silver flame on a cloud of black smoke twisted like a spun dagger and disappeared beyond the trees fringing the river. A booming crash sent the cats scuttling beneath chairs. She called Patrick. 'I think a plane has crashed.'

'Dear God,' he said. He held up a book. 'I was reading this when I heard the explosion: "I know that I shall meet my fate Somewhere among the clouds above."'

The summer before I started at Mary Hall, Brodie and Flook went to Scotland on their own to stay with Mummy's sister. I was supposed to go too, but I couldn't bear to miss a whole week of mucking out and riding. The house was very big and quiet without the boys, and the cupboards, usually empty within hours of Mummy's weekly shopping trip, bulged with food. Daddy, Mummy, Dan, Poppy and I all went to meet Brodie and Flook at the station, leaving the table laid and decorated for a celebratory supper on their return.

The train from Scotland, shrieking and steaming, drew in to the platform as dusk fell. Carriage windows glowed yellow and welcoming in a long string, like the amber necklace my great-grandmother had given me. We wobbled on tiptoe at the gate, craning to see the boys get off. The last passengers, the very old and the very young, were wheeled past us in their chairs and still the boys didn't come. Daddy walked down the platform sticking his head into every door of the train. He disappeared into a distant carriage and came out carrying Flook.

Mummy thrust Poppy at me. 'Wait here.' She ran towards Daddy. Dan clutched my leg, Poppy slipped in my arms and

I was afraid. Mummy was running fast down the platform but dread made it seem as if she was moving in slow motion. Brodie was behind Daddy now, they were coming slowly, so slowly. Brodie dragged the suitcase, straining with the effort. All I could see of Flook was his pale face framed by tousled hair and still far away. He was so white I thought his head was covered by a handkerchief.

Tears spilt from Dan's eyes and trickled down his cheeks. 'Is Flook dead?' he whispered.

I gripped his hand tightly. 'I don't know.'

Flook, looking no heavier than a curved leaf in Daddy's arms, and Mummy with Brodie, reached us. Flook groaned.

'He's not dead. Hooray!' Dan jumped rhythmically in his red wellingtons.

'He's very ill,' said Mummy. 'We have to take him to hospital now.' Brodie hid his face in Mummy's collar. His long arms were doubled around her shoulders but he was too big for her to carry. In the car I held his hand. 'We were playing cards on the train and eating the sandwiches Aunt Fanny made us. Then Flook started screaming about his tummy hurting. The guard came and he couldn't stop him crying. I think we were near Norwich because the guard sent a lady to sit with us and then we were here. Flook has been crying all the time and Mummy says it's his appendix. He didn't even know who I was.'

Brodie's face was grey, his eyes twitched with tiredness as he spoke. He shuddered, gripping my hand. 'I thought he was dying. I was so scared.' His voice was tiny now. 'I knew it was my fault he was dying. He must have had a bad sandwich and I should have eaten it. I'm the eldest when you aren't there.'

I hugged him, tears smarting. 'No, Brodie. Appendixes don't come from bad sandwiches, they come from germs or something. He will be fine in hospital and it's not your fault at all.' Brodie sniffed. He was not convinced.

At the hospital Mummy went in with Flook, Daddy spun the car out of the car park and roared home with us. He ran into the house leaving the headlights on and the door open. The engine gurgled and stopped. We followed slowly. Daddy was on the phone.

'It is damnable. The poor child is in agony. I must go back.' He stopped speaking and hugged Brodie. 'Louise is coming down to look after you all. I must go back to your Mummy and Flook.' He paced around the rush matting of the room, a cigarette cupped in his hand; we watched in a doleful row.

'Louise will be here in a minute,' I said to him. 'Go now.' He looked doubtful.

'Go on, Daddy.' Brodie dropped on to his knees by the fire, leaning his face against Honey, the lissom blonde labrador we had found as an unspectacular replacement for Dobe. And Daddy was gone.

Louise lived opposite the church at the top of the hill in the village. Her house had once been a blacksmith's forge and we hid in the mouth of an ancient hearth when we played there with Louise's sons. If we stayed to tea, Louise made chips in a thick grey saucepan full of foaming oil. We clamoured for more, stuffing ourselves because we never had chips at home.

Louise arrived as the headlights of Daddy's car swept up the hill and out of the village. 'Oh, how nice this all looks,' she said, seeing the kitchen table laid and the big card I had made to welcome the boys home. 'You poor loves. Don't worry, Flook will be fine. Mummy will ring up soon to tell you how he is.' She reached her arms out and like eager puppies we scrambled towards her.

Louise gave us supper. We had some of the chicken pie Mummy had made, and then she took Dan and Poppy up to bed. Brodie and I lay in front of the fire, our heads pillowed by Honey's soft bulk, and watched television.

At nine o'clock the telephone rang. It was Daddy. 'Darling heart, Flook is sleeping soundly. He had to have an operation but now he is much better. I will be home to you soon. Mummy is staying the night here with Flook.'

Hot tears spilt down my face. 'Thank goodness he's not going to die.' Louise made us cocoa and we dragged ourselves up to bed. For comfort we each took a kitten; Angelica and Witton curled themselves in our beds like hot-water bottles and purred sympathy through the night.

Flook was ill for a long time. Something went wrong after his operation and Daddy had to drive back in the middle of the night. Louise came down to look after us in her nightdress. Flook nearly died and we gleaned enough terrible information to become hysterical. No one explained.

'Please tell me what's happening,' I begged Louise. She had slept all night by the telephone; her ankles gleamed cold white in the morning. 'He'll be all right, don't you worry,' was all she would say.

Flook stayed in hospital in a room of his own and his face shrank as his hair grew. He looked like a bush-baby or a sweet little monkey, eyes huge in his papery face, arms thin, wrists protruding towards sharp simian paws. Mummy stayed with him, and every day Daddy took us to visit them. We were never allowed to stay long as Flook became tired very easily. Daddy sat with him and told him stories while Mummy took us out into Norwich. We went to the Castle Museum to see the stuffed animals. Contained in glass cases, huge tigers and lions stood arrested mid-snarl, glaring at our faces flattened against their barricade. Brodie found a black button sunk into a post and pressed it without thinking. The gallery filled with growls and roars. Poppy squeaked, 'Help, Mummy, help!' and wrapped herself in Mummy's coat. Brodie froze, for a split second thinking he had brought the animals to life.

'Turn them off,' Dan begged, 'I don't like it.' His round face was woebegone inside his green corduroy hood and he stamped his foot as the lion roared. 'Stop that, you silly cat,' he shouted.

We moved on to the Egyptian section. 'Cleopatra was the Queen of Egypt,' Mummy told Dan and Poppy. 'She was very beautiful, with raven-black hair and milk-white skin. She kept herself beautiful by bathing in asses' milk.'

'Yuck,' said Brodie. 'It must have smelt disgusting.'

Dan was fascinated. 'Did she drink from her bath before she washed or after?'

I stopped in front of a tiny bound casket and looked in horror. 'Mummy, it's a cat, a poor little cat. Look what they've done to it.' The others rushed to see and Dan burst into tears. 'Will Flook look like that soon?'

'No, darling, of course he won't. Flook is much better now.' Mummy's hair was standing on end in static wisps as she tried to keep us all from becoming hysterical. 'The Egyptians wrapped up their very special animals in these bandages when they died, and then they buried them in great tombs. You know about mummies, don't you? Well, this is a mummified cat.'

P atrick loved wrestling. Brought up in a tenement block in Chelsea, he had learnt little at school save how to dodge the blackboard rubber which his angry teacher threw around the class of forty naughty infants. He fought then in street scuffles, and, when he grew up, in bars and pubs from here to Nagasaki. His anger dwindled, and at Mildney wrestling was an armchair sport. He watched it every Saturday with the boys. Giant Haystacks and Big Daddy were his favourites and he leaned towards the screen, searching with his hand for the ashtray in the gloom of the playroom. He always shut the curtains when he was watching television.

'Marvellous. It's fiendish, almost Chinese.' No praise could be higher, and he nudged Flook to attention as two fat thugs splattered one another across the ring.

Patrick mended bikes with copper wire and masking tape and endless optimism. He and his brother had built cars together as young men. They raced one across Texas once with the Earl of Dunlane.

Va Va wobbled off on her bicycle. 'That's dandy,' said Patrick, but she tumbled a moment later when the injured wheel buckled again. His spanner set was prized beyond anything he owned. Wrath gathered in an instant cloud if any went missing. 'One of you has stolen it.' He glared round the yard. 'You can damn well find it or else . . .' Flook ran up to him and pulled the spanner from the pocket of Patrick's jeans. Fury vanished. 'Cleverest bambino, you deserve a prize.' And reaching for his cigarette packet, Patrick pulled out the silver foil and made a tiny goblet for Flook. 'This is the cup that the Knights of the Round Table drank from,' he said.

'No it's not. You just made it.'

Patrick looked down his long nose. 'It is magic, young man.' Flook howled with laughter, bent double over his crumpled goblet.

D addy was very upset by Flook's illness. He usually only went into the Drinking Room on Saturdays, but while Mummy was at the hospital he drifted in every evening and stood, shoulders hunched, staring into the cold fireplace. Louise left her children with her mother and came to look after us, but I thought Daddy needed more care. I peered through the crack in the door at dusk, worried that he might be lonely. He was looking out towards the river, one arm raised to the top of the window frame. Through the small panes of glass clouds bowled across a sky dark with approaching storms. Daddy turned round and saw me. 'Come in, my love, come in.' The Drinking Room seemed forlorn with just Daddy and no fire lit, and although I hated drinking evenings, I wished Daddy had someone there to cheer him up.

'Daddy, are you all right?'

He smiled and pulled me over to him. 'I'm keeping company with Bacchus and some old ghosts,' he said. 'I miss your Mummy.'

I sat down in a deep armchair. 'She'll be back soon.' I curled up and leaned my cheek against the soft density of velvet. 'Flook really is getting better now, isn't he?'

Daddy poured a splash of Martini and some water into his glass and raised it. 'Yes, thank Christ. He is better. But he has paid with the loss of innocence.'

Louise came in. 'Now Patrick, what stories are you telling this poor child?' She sounded a little flirtatious, deliberately light-hearted, like all Mummy's friends when they talked to Daddy.

Daddy looked at her and didn't speak. He drank some Martini and still he didn't speak. He winked at me. 'A tiny discussion about Life and Love and the great Hereafter,' he said in his most professorial tones.

Louise laughed. 'Well, it's supper-time, so come and have some spaghetti.'

'Dear God, these women are frightening,' Daddy whispered to me as we followed Louise. 'But what can I do? Your Mummy has left her orders, and we must obey her.'

June 1986

B rodie and Flook became taller than Dad without anyone noticing them grow. They were stringy and clumsy, and nearly twenty. Their huge feet tripped people over in the kitchen where they sat at the table whistling and fidgeting, waiting like cuckoos for Mum to give them breakfast. I watched them from my distant pinnacle of London glamour, home for a weekend and frothing my conversation with stories of champagne and film stars I had encountered at parties. I was twenty-one and liberated; a friend of a friend had got me a job with a small television production company and suddenly, by accident, I was a real person. The boys, jeans ripped, housed in West London squats, regarded me curiously, their smiles indulgent and conspiratorial as I rattled on. 'Get her,' Brodie grinned when I advanced into the kitchen, prancing in a swish of lemon-sorbet silk. 'This dress is borrowed from a fashion designer,' I boasted. 'We used it for a programme on couture last week. Do you like it?'

'It's all right.' Brodie lit a cigarette and rolled back on his chair. 'You do look a bit of a prat, though.'

I scowled and spun out of the kitchen. Dad was in the

playroom, small in the arms of a big chair. A book lay open, rising and falling gently on his stomach, resting with him while he slept. He looked up as I opened the door. 'Enchanting, dear heart, and utterly frivolous.'

As the boys grew, Dad seemed to shrink. Brown pill-bottles and little inhalers like periscopes appeared in the house and followed him wherever he went. He coughed a lot, and when I asked him what he wanted me to bring from London he looked solemn and said, 'A pair of wings for when I go to join the angels.'

'What do you mean?' My voice, intended to be bantering and no-nonsense, quavered on a sob.

Dad leaned forward and winked in conspiracy. 'Get me a cigarette, kid, and don't tell your mother. The doctor thinks I've given up, and Ellie's been policing me.'

A sheet of ice slid between my skin and the swathed warmth of silk. He was really ill. He was about to die, I was never going to see him again. I knew that, in years, he was old enough to be our grandfather, but in spirit he was younger than all my friends' parents. His mortality hit me coldly in the face. My nose prickled and began to run as tears swelled in my eyes. Miserable, guilty, I gave Dad a cigarette from my packet. How could I refuse his final request? Mum came in, bringing a cup of tea and a piece of dark, wet cake for Dad.

'Where did you get that cigarette?' she demanded, and my face crumpled in a weeping slide.

'Dad said he wanted one last one,' I gulped, wiping streaming eyes on the hem of my dress, and followed her out of the room. 'Why didn't you tell me?'

Mum looked blank. 'Tell you what?'

'How ill Dad is.' I was off. Trembling, exploding with sobs, smearing black drips of mascara down my peerless, priceless, borrowed yellow dress.

I heard Mum laughing, soothing, close to my ear as she stroked my hair. 'Pay no attention to him at all,' she insisted. 'He's been ill, and Dr Jones wants him to stop smoking, but he's as strong as an ox, and as stubborn. He particularly enjoys getting cigarettes by blackmail, and even had a bet with Flook about how many he would achieve today.'

Relief turned to outrage. I marched back into the playroom. 'How could you, Dad. Look what's happened to my dress, all because you had some stupid bet with Flook.' I flashed the damp skirt towards him and he bowed his head and looked sheepish. 'Why can't that goddam woman mind her own business,' he said out of the corner of his mouth.

But later, he stood up very slowly and paused to catch his breath before leaving the room. I glanced at Brodie stretched full length on the sofa, black boots lolling on the rocking-horse beyond. He was watching Dad, and his expression was lopsided and dismayed.

Neither of the cars was working on my first day at Mary Hall's School. Louise offered to drive me to school and Mummy, with Poppy in tow, came too. We sat in a row on the front seat of Louise's pea-green camper van. Mummy and Louise chattered and laughed, Poppy slept, and I clenched my teeth and gazed out of the window, trying to plot an escape from the camper van at an invisible distance from the school.

I had never had a school uniform before, nor indeed a whole outfit of new clothes. Daddy took me to Norwich armed with a pale-green list of school requirements and we bought them all. On the school outfitting floor of Blond's department store we hailed a matronly woman. She had frizzy grey hair and a badge with 'Madge Wilkins' written on it. Madge had never met anyone like my father.

'My dear lady.' He leaned on the counter and pushed his dark glasses on to his forehead. 'Would you be kind enough to render us assistance in dressing my daughter as befits a pupil of Mary Hall's School?' He lowered his glasses again and lit a cigarette. Madge patted her hair and overlooked the cigarette. She led us to a rail of drab green clothes. Daddy removed his glasses for a closer look. 'Remarkable,' he drawled. 'Do you think they deliberately dress these poor children like lesbian aunts, or is it done through ignorance?'

Madge bridled. 'Mary Hall's is the most expensive uniform on our racks,' she reproved.

'Dear God,' said Daddy, 'let's get this damn thing over, then.'

Madge reached into shelves and boxes and brought out cream shirts, fawn jerseys, socks, and bile-green heaps of skirt and blazer. Daddy became bored before we got to ties and gym knickers and left me, speechless and bewildered, by the pile of my acquisitions.

'I don't really like that,' I said. Madge was holding up a jersey the colour and texture of thick porridge. 'Do I have to have it?'

Madge clucked like a broody hen as she consulted the list. She pulled out a thin, tawny cardigan. It reminded me of Ginger, Brodie's cat, and I nodded. 'That one is fine. I can wear it under my jacket when I go riding.'

But there was no alternative to the foul skirt, a triangle of crackling synthetic fabric. Madge insisted on one several sizes too big. Its folds reached half-way down my calves and hung there, inelegant and stiff, like mildewed cardboard. 'It's a polyester mix,' enthused Madge, 'so Mum can just pop it in the washing machine and run a cool iron over it.'

I thought of Mummy's iron, its once shiny surface blackened and ploughed where Daddy had used it to press masking tape on to his torn jeans. 'We haven't got a washing machine.'

Madge gasped. Her face registered the tragic pity she would have displayed if I had told her I had no mother.

Daddy returned. 'Dear lady' – he leaned on the pile of uniform in front of Madge – 'could she not have one of those black dresses that the divine Goldie wears on *Top of the Pops*? Are you with me? The dress is, I think, made from a black plastic bag.'

'She's not called Goldie,' I hissed at him. 'She's called Blondie.'

Madge knew who he meant. 'My sons love her,' she beamed, showing white, even dentures between her frosted lips. 'You might find those frocks on the fashion floor, but I'm not sure that we stock them.'

Daddy nodded sagely. 'Ah so,' he said.

We took the clothes to the cash desk and they were priced. I was mortified when the total was rung up. 'Daddy, we can't afford sixty pounds,' I whispered, 'we'll be bankrupt.'

'My love, I will be the judge of that. But it does seem a shame that your uniform should be so uniform. Let us go and buy a pen.'

We bought a beautiful silver pen and an atlas. We didn't buy the regulation green Bible because Daddy leafed through it. 'This is rubbish. You will read the King James Bible, if – which I doubt – you read the Bible at all.'

I was worried. 'But Daddy, what will I do in scripture lessons?'

'You will not attend them,' he said firmly. 'You are a Catholic and you have no need of scripture lessons.'

Daddy never went to church, and when I asked him if I was going to be confirmed, he said, 'There is no reason for you to confirm your faith, just as there is no reason for you to confess to it.'

October 1986

L ondon was fun for me but not for my cats. Angelica and Witton sat on the high windowsills of my flat, looking out at treetops in the communal gardens behind. Guilt followed me out of the door when I went to work each day leaving a floor deep in clothes. The cats padded through the chaos, flexing luxuriating claws, then curling up plump in the folds of a dressing-gown until I returned. However stealthily I made my late-night entrance, they woke, purring machine-gun joy, twisting and cloying round my legs while I poured them milk. My dependants. The guilt turned to panic when one of Witton's ears began to droop forward, like a shattered traffic bollard. I rang Mum and found a cardboard box. In went Witton, one ear twitching, the other at half-mast; in went Angelica, a ball of struggling orange fury. I drove them to the station and waved them off on the train like a mother abandoning her children to a new term at boarding-school.

Mum rang me that evening. 'Darling, those poor cats, they look utterly miserable. Something's happened to Witton's ear. They miss you. I don't know if it will work having them here. When are you coming down to visit them? And us?'

But there never seemed to be time. Every day I went to work, proudly arranging myself at my desk and making a hundred vital phone calls. Every evening I went to a party, or two, or three, chattering and bustling through unnoticed changing seasons as I plunged into London.

Brodie and Flook were in London too, but they didn't have telephones. Sometimes they turned up in Covent Garden at the office, and I brought them up to my department for a cup of coffee, half embarrassed by their torn, faded clothes but ablaze with pride at the lingering looks from the other girls.

One day Brodie arrived at lunch-time. He was wearing a suit, and his hair was smooth, slicked black, a yellow strand from his peroxide days bleached stiff behind his ear. 'I've got a job in the City,' he said. 'I'm selling bonds. I'll take you out to lunch if you like.'

He wasn't my little brother any more, striding now in grey pinstripes, his hat low on his brow like Bugsy Malone. We went to a Greek restaurant. 'When did you last go home?' he asked, reaching for a cigarette.

'I haven't been for ages.' I didn't look at him as I spoke. I knew he wasn't smiling.

'You should go. Dad isn't well, you know, winter is coming, and he hates it, especially when the clocks go back. It would really cheer him up to see you.'

I was defensive. 'I saw him the other day when he came to get that prize. You were there, you know I did.'

'That's different. One drunken evening with thousands of people isn't like going home, is it?'

I twisted my fork in the crumbly mound of feta cheese on my

plate; an olive dropped out and rolled on to the floor. I felt sick and scared. Brodie was irritating me with his superior manner. 'What about you, then? You only go when you need money, and you won't need money now, so I suppose you want me to go instead of you.'

Before the flash of anger in his eyes I saw panic and fear, and I was angry too. Why should we have to look after our parents? Why should we have to worry about them? Small and sad, Brodie and I sat at the Formica table, food untouched, ashtray full, a dreadful shared, unspoken fear heavy in the air between us.

Louise parked the embarrassing green van outside the school. We were late, so no little girls stood gazing curiously and sniggering as I arrived. Mummy took me in and handed me over to Miss Neilson, whose browny-red face and knot of white hair reminded me of an onion.

My new school was wonderful. Light bow-windowed classrooms, different coloured exercise books for each subject, a huge playing-field surrounded by chestnut trees, order and punctuality, and best of all, girls. I had never experienced undiluted female company before. I frisked in the soft scented air which surrounded the sixth-formers, and studiously copied the fourth-form fashions in folders and satchels.

On the first day at Rec, the new name I had to learn for playtime, I sat stiff at my desk, willing someone to come and talk to me but at the same time praying for invisibility to observe the bonds of friendship forming between the others. A sturdy girl with the face of a refined bull terrier approached. 'I've seen you at Pony Club,' she said, and I cringed. I recognized her from a day when Shalimar demolished the doughnut stand at a horse show and Mummy laughed so much that she lay down on the grass next to him, her dress beaded with sugar from the doughnuts. Humiliated by both pet and parent, I had walked away from the scene.

'I'm Amelia Letson,' continued the bull terrier. Searching her face for mockery, I found none, and replied, 'I'm Gabriella Lincoln.'

Another girl, big-boned, blonde, skin the colour of rich cream, moved towards us. 'Hello. You ride at my aunt's stables, don't you? I've seen you when I've been to tea at Grandma's house.' I recognized her as Sasha Warton and smiled gratefully. We talked about ponies until a bell shrilled in our ears and classes began again.

Each day, after assembly in the hall where wafts of lunch and beeswax polish mingled with teachers' scent and pupils' nail varnish and hairspray, I examined my timetable. Terrified of being late, I ran to the classrooms. The chemistry lab was my favourite room in the school even though I was not good at science. High mahogany tables ran in rows and on each table Bunsen burners were umbilically tethered to hidden gas pipes by yellow tubes. Test tubes gleamed in neat ranks, half-filled with peacock-bright crystals of blue, violet and sulphurous yellow.

Chemistry was like cooking in a well-ordered kitchen but more fun. My chocolate-brown chemistry exercise books were immaculate. I relished their pristine perfection and lost marks for writing on only one side of the page. I left the facing page blank because it looked nice. At the beginning of my third year, the school opened a new three-storey science block and I lost interest in chemistry. The subject had no charm when we sat at plastic-topped desks and worked at low white benches round the wall. The brown exercise books became blotched and crumpled like all the rest of my work, and I found no pleasure in mixing formulas. The possibility of inventing Frankenstein's monster had evaporated like burnt-off copper sulphate in the new sterile surroundings.

Briefly inspired by botany, I made a garden at Mildney. I dug a small patch by the kitchen wall and planted it with mint and tulips. Each day I weeded and tended my patch, ganning satisfaction from the regimental rows of flowers and my manicured expanse of earth. It was a hazardous pastime. The path leading from my garden to the back yard was the boundary of the conceited cockerel Cedric's province, and its prettiness belied the danger lurking in the lupins. Cedric was a bantam. He had long russet feathers which glistened copper and green when he preened. He had a blood-red comb as plump as an ear lobe and a very high opinion of himself.

But like all braggadocios, Cedric was a coward. Camouflaged, he hid in the flower-beds awaiting his victims, the amber bead of his eye glowing malevolently from the foliage. He watched me toiling in my garden and, when my back was turned, sprang, neck extended and wings akimbo. His hooked beak jabbed my ear, his horny spurs scrabbled against my spine and I screamed and ran for the back door. Cedric let go and vanished, a ball of fire tumbling into a distant clump of nettles where he knew he was safe.

Brodie came out with a stick to chase him but Cedric crouched invisible until Brodie turned his back and then he repeated the ambush. He was Brodie's bird, but he ignored the rules of fealty and attacked his master as much as anyone else. He deserved a gruesome punishment, but the massacre effected by the dogs was too great a price to pay.

Returning from a family outing we bumped up the drive, opening the doors of the car before it had stopped. I ran to greet Honey and my puppy, Miriam. They were newly back from the muck heap. 'Ugh, you dogs stink.' I edged past them towards the field. Looking back at the house, I noticed dark bundles littered across the grass, inert heaps which from a distance looked like stones. I approached one and gasped. It was Cilla Black, the mother of the Pop Stars, one of our bantam families. Cilla Black's beady yellow eyes were closed, her beak was half open and her little pink tongue protruded pathetically. She lay, her neck twisted awkwardly on the glistening black bulk of her body, dead but still warm. A few yards away, Gary Glitter and Rod Stewart, a pair of young roosters who had been inseparable in life, were heaped together in death, their long tail-feathers trailing like a widow's weeds.

I stood appalled, my mouth a screaming square. No one came. No one came. From all over the garden I heard the shrilling yells and bellows of my brothers as they discovered more corpses. Mummy was crouched over something by the washing line. Leaning over, I saw what she was looking at. Emerald the tame hen, who laid her eggs on the doormat for our convenience and ate from our hands, gently, not with the darting movements which frightened small children, lay panting and trembling at Mummy's feet. Relief washed over me. At least one of them was alive.

Mummy was crying. 'Those bloody dogs. Those *bloody* dogs.' Miriam loped up, kissed Mummy with her soft tongue and whisked off again.

'I think she was saying sorry,' I said.

'Don't you believe it.' Mummy's tone was grim. 'She's deranged. Honey would never have done this. It's all that puppy's doing.'

We took Emerald into the coal shed and made her a bed on Flook's anorak. We gave her bread and milk and she fluffed up her feathers and regained her low crooning voice. Daddy appeared in the door of the shed with a spade. 'I'm going to shoot those goddam dogs,' he muttered, 'but first we must bury the dead.' He stomped off to dig a grave. Brodie and Flook, a drooping hen under each arm, trailed after him to the Wilderness. Twenty-five hens died. Only Emerald and Cedric, whose cowardice had protected him, survived. Cedric was roosting high up in the lime tree squawking hoarsely every two minutes as though he had been hypnotized. He did not come down until the next day. The hens had been frightened to death by Miriam's game. She pranced and barked around each one, whipped into further hysteria by the flying feathers and squawks as the poor foolish hens ran round in circles trying to escape.

Mummy said we had to give Miriam away, and sadly I agreed. She could not go on living in a house with hens, even dead hens. Miriam was taken. Mummy felt a twinge of conscience as she was driven off by her proud new owners, a pair of pigeon-fanciers from Wisbech whom we had told nothing of her crime.

Emerald recovered but the shock had affected her hormones.

Hearing a strangled cry a few days later, I ran out and found her perched on a log trying to crow. Every day she ritualistically made the attempt and, as her crowing improved, long tail-feathers sprouted and her comb grew raspberry red and large like Cedric's. In three months her transformation was complete and Emerald became a cockerel, a fit sparring partner for the insufferable Cedric.

Patrick loved getting up early and he made runny porridge on the Aga. Va Va heard loud classical music blare from the wireless on the kitchen windowsill and ran down to beg Patrick to draw faces on her porridge with trickles of golden syrup. The children knew that Patrick was susceptible to a certain look, eyes wide and innocent.

'Daddy, can we have biscuits for pudding and then go and buy some sweets at Mr Cardew's?'

'Anything, loves, anything,' he agreed absently, leaning over the white, cold washbasin in the cloakroom as he shaved.

After breakfast he kissed their sticky faces and shut himself in the study. The children knew they must not disturb him, but would creep to the door and crouch outside on the flagstones, listening as he played back poems he had read into a tape recorder. He sounded different when he talked to them, and Va Va asked why.

Patrick looked grave, but he winked and said, 'Now my love, you are getting serious.' She had no idea what he meant.

The study was exciting. It was warm and smelt of cigarettes; it was usually forbidden territory, piled high with books and papers. Va Va sat on Patrick's knee and talked into the tape recorder while Brodie wrote wispy letters in a notebook. Patrick liked the children's interruptions, but one day, when the milkman, the man who drove the Sunshine Bread van and the butcher had all waved cheery good-mornings to him through the window, he took his books and his green chair upstairs and made the big spare room his study.

He hated talking to anyone during the day. He once went to the village shop, and only once. Mr Cardew, the shopkeeper, jaunty in his Camp Coffee apron, greeted him with delight. 'Mr Lincoln, come for some gaspers, have you?' He rubbed his hands together, beaming. 'Can't write those poems without something to light the fire, can we?' and he cackled mightily.

Patrick was horrified. He never went to the shop again, but drove five miles to Aylthorpe to buy his cigarettes.

Sasha Warton and I were in the same stream for all classes. To my relief we became friends in the maths class, where my confusion at the problems set was as deep as my surprise at finding myself in division one. For a time my academic career flourished, and I played in the lacrosse team and swam in the swimming team. I conceived a satisfactory notion of myself as prefect material, and sustained it by always standing up when staff came into a room and by smiling winningly at anyone who addressed me.

Sasha's parents were divorced. She lived with her mother during the week, in a small, very clean house near the school. Sometimes I stayed the night with her, revelling in the decadence of central heating and a duvet on the bed. Best of all I avoided the long bus journey home and the punishing dawn rush to catch the bus to school from Aylthorpe. I was envious of Sasha's ordered existence. At weekends, her father collected her from school and drove her to his house. It was near Mildney, so he dropped me off on the way. This was a big worry. Mummy told me it was polite to ask him in, so I did, every time. He always said no, but I was terrified that one day he would say yes, and see how very different our kitchen was from the shiny bright new one I had seen in his house.

Richard Warton was the only son of Lord and Lady Warton. He lived in a moated red-brick mansion a mile from Mildney and drove a blue sports car. An admirer of the arts, he filled the medieval rooms of his house with contemporary paintings, and textiles woven from the wool of his own sheep. He invited my father to give a reading there. Mummy and Daddy took me with them, and we arrived at Felt Hall in Mummy's mini-van, puffing black billows of smoke like a smouldering dragon. I was very pleased that my parents were visiting a school friend's parents, but my knees shook with fear in case Daddy shouted at Richard Warton. In the Great Hall Mummy and I pressed together, embarrassed and nervous in the yawning space. We moved towards a wall, its polished panelling scarred by deep scratches. I traced my fingers down the wounds, imagining marauding knights hundreds of years ago.

Beside us was an open fireplace surrounded by delicate blue and white tiles, and in the near distance a squad of grey plastic chairs huddled in the middle of the flagstoned floor. Daddy sat at a table facing the chairs. Whispering and scraping the floor, a tide of scrubbed women and overweight men seeped on to the chairs, corduroy-covered bottoms overflowing. Others, hesitating over where to sit, caused an eddy in the stream before plunging to a chair stranded on the perimeter of the group. Some of these people I recognized as other parents from school, and pride, mixed with resentment at their gazing at Daddy as though he were an exhibit, choked my lungs.

Richard Warton sat next to Daddy at the little table, leaning towards him and talking while people sat down. I watched Daddy's face anxiously, waiting for his brow to furrow and his mouth to turn down at one corner in anger. But he was laughing. He put his cigarette out in his glass. Richard leapt up to find him an ashtray.

When all the chairs were full, and some people were standing at the back, Richard stood up. His grey wavy hair curled down to his shoulders, and he wore brown plus-fours and thick patterned socks. He looked like Lord Emsworth showing off the Empress of Blandings. Mummy and I, sitting together at the front, giggled nervously.

'We are delighted to have with us this evening Patrick Lincoln, one of the greatest poets of this century. Many of you may know him already as a neighbour, for Patrick lives a mile from here at Mildney with his family,' and Richard beamed a big-toothed white smile and sat down.

Daddy stood up. He came round to the front of the table, leaned against it and crossed his feet. 'This is a beautiful house,' he said. 'Now let's get this reading lark over and done with. I shall read to you from a new poem.' Daddy reached into the top pocket of his jacket and took out a notebook. The audience tittered uneasily, stopping abruptly when Daddy raised his cupped hand to shoulder height. He began to read.

Daddy's voice thundered, echoing across the room. He glared at the page he was reading, and his words rolled slowly out. He read for a long time, perhaps twenty minutes, from one poem, and no one moved or sneezed or scratched. When he stopped, I found my nose and eyes smarting with tears. Daddy stared across the room. There was silence, then clapping began, and although there were no more than fifty people, the clapping was a crescendoed roar. Daddy and Richard left the table and walked through into the next room.

'I can't believe he read that poem here,' Mummy whispered to me. 'He said he was going to read some children's poems and one or two about Norfolk.'

'Perhaps he thought it was a good place to practise it,' I whispered back. 'Do you think they understood it? I didn't.'

'It doesn't matter if they did or not,' said Mummy, crouching beside me and reaching beneath the chair for her bag. 'Your father wants people to listen to and enjoy his poems; he never cares if they understand them or not.'

I listened to the comments around us. 'Quite remarkable, I need a drink after that'; 'Never heard anything like it, what did Richard say his name was?'

A woman I had never seen before, with a strident, horsy voice, was proudly announcing, 'Patrick and his wife Eleanor are great friends of ours. Of course, the man's a genius.' I craned, hoping the woman might add, 'Charming children, inherited his genius apparently,' but she was gurgling with echoing laughter at something her consort had said.

'Well, everyone here enjoyed it,' I whispered back to Mummy. 'They didn't move for twenty minutes.' I stood up, my pride in Daddy making me feel tall, sophisticated and confident.

A cream carpet as thick as a lawn lay across the drawing-room floor and the walls were spattered with paintings of black blobs. Daddy leaned against the mantelpiece, talking to a woman with thin red hair. She was smoking a pipe.

'Are you, in fact, a man? Could you be the reincarnation of my great hero Sherlock Holmes?' I heard him ask her, and my ballooning pride deflated.

The woman laughed. 'No. This is a pipe, not a way of life. I'm married to Richard, actually.'

'Ah, well, Holmes would never have done that, would he?' A martial light sparked in Daddy's eye. Mummy, tilting a glass of wine precariously towards the carpet, struggled through the tightly knit mob to his side.

'Let's get the hell out of here, Ellie. I will not talk to these people,' he whispered to her. But Mummy was talking to Richard's wife, asking about their recent wedding, encouraging her to make light of Daddy's remarks. Mummy leaned on a small wooden table and sipped her wine. A man with grey hair came up to Daddy and asked him to sign a book. Mummy and Sonia, the wife, were talking about roses, their voices melting in the cloud of conversation and smoke. A splintering crash broke like ice across the room. The tiny table Mummy had been leaning on collapsed, and she and her glass of red wine spilt on to the creamy carpet. Her black-clad legs splayed against pale fluff; next to her a wine-dark pool seeped. Mummy didn't know what to apologize for or what to try and salvage. The table was a heap of jagged wood. I felt her embarrassment as Sonia poured salt over the carpet, and it reached me over my own hot-faced humiliation.

Daddy laughed, one huge 'Ha ha', and knocked back his own wine, saying gently, 'Eleanor, Eleanor, when will you learn to behave?' He took Mummy's hand, smiling as he turned to Richard. 'I must apologize for my wife, and to cover her shame with a veil of diplomacy I shall take her home.' He was laughing, and Mummy, wet with wine and speechless with mortification, mumbled 'Of course we will pay for the table' as we left. I hung my head, blushing, too humiliated to catch anyone's eye.

Outside, stars swooped low in the black autumn sky and the air was heavy with the dank reptilian scent of the moat. 'Your Mummy is wonderful,' Daddy said to me as we got into the car. 'She got us out of there in less than five minutes, and what's more, we won't be asked back.' He was gleeful, driving very fast along the tiny lanes, the headlamps cleaving a path between dark, heaped hedges.

At home, the boys were watching television and Marmalade had knocked over a bottle of milk in the kitchen, purring with deep satisfaction as her pink tongue lapped up the puddle on the table. Mummy relaxed and laughed too when Daddy told the story to the boys, and I was left lonely, washed up on a dirty shore of embarrassment from which I longed to be rescued.

On a hot summer morning, Dad arrived at my front door in London wearing dark glasses and carrying a small black suitcase. He looked suntanned and healthy, and it was hard to believe that he had ever been ill.

'Have you got a passport?' he asked.

I made tea and took it on to the balcony with its view of cars inching along the A40. 'Yes, why?'

He looked at his watch. 'We have precisely two hours before the plane leaves for Rome. I should like to take you with me.'

Scattering clothes and toothbrushes, books and shoes, I spiralled around the flat, packing nonsense in my excitement. Dad had been invited to read at the Rome Poetry Festival, and Mum was too afraid of flying to go with him. I was on my way to Rome for the first time since infancy.

We arrived at the Hotel George Washington in time for a silvered sorbet in the walled garden. We sat in the shade of a faded pink umbrella, and Dad lifted his sunglasses from his nose and beamed his delight. 'This is the nearest you or I will ever get to heaven,' he said. I squirmed with pleasure, happy to be in Rome with my father, doing the sort of thing that other people did. We took a taxi and walked through the still, hot gardens of the Villa Giulia where twisted pines and plush cypress trees canopied us, suffocating the blaring horns and screeching brakes of Rome.

In the evening we went to watch athletics. It was dark when we reached Mussolini's stadium. Neo-classical statues surrounded the arena, lit blue and holy by tungsten arc lights. We ate hot dogs and drank beer, squashed together on a bench in the midst of pooping hooters and wildly excited Italians. Looking down at the cinder-red track where athletes pranced and jogged, I shivered with the presence of long ago, when gladiators fought to the death. I was choosing a random athlete to throw to the lions when Dad gripped my arm. 'Look, there he is. It's Moses.' A towering, gleaming man, his skin polished mink-dark, skipped and hopped past. The crowd surged, rolling to its feet to honour the American hurdler, and Dad sat rapt, silent.

A starting-pistol cracked, and Moses floated over a chain of white hurdles, tilting his long body forward. Over the line, he flashed a wide white smile and three girls behind me screamed a fanfare of bliss. Dad was as carried away as they were, tears coursing down his face as he clapped and clapped.

The poetry reading took place at sunset on the following evening. In a glade in a garden a great platform had been erected. A row of poets sat drinking to one side, swaying on their seats like a throng of sea-lions. At a spotlit lectern a blonde with heaving *décolletage* introduced them in breathless Italian. Dad stood up; the other sea-lions bayed approval. He moved to the lectern and read his poems in English. When he stopped, red roses rained on him from the applauding audience. Dad

81

picked one up and gave it to the blonde, who pressed it down into her cleavage. Everyone liked that. The poets clapped and the crowd cheered. I crumpled in my seat, and realized how nervous I had been.

Dad was having dinner with an old friend, a tall blind poet with the hooked nose and white face of a snowy owl. They took me with them to a tiny restaurant and I became very drunk. They did not notice until we left, when I stumbled helplessly. Dad and his friend grasped an elbow each and pulled me home, their walking-sticks tapping an accompaniment to our weaving progress.

In the morning, Dad was unsympathetic about my throbbing head. 'Poor love,' he said. 'But you know, it happens to everyone the first time they come to Rome. It's the air as much as the wine.' He scarcely looked up from his paper and his foaming coffee. 'To cleanse your soul we shall visit some churches today.' I ate a brioche, a taste of almond air, and suppressed my self-pity.

Dad and I flew back to London after a day spent between the Etruscan Museum in the Villa Giulia and La Rinascente, a jewel of a department store. As a souvenir I had a black bikini; Dad had a tiny Etruscan statue with a vast penis.

It was Saturday. Brodie and Flook, who had now joined him at King Henry's School, met us at the bus-stop in Norwich after lessons and Dad drove us all to Liza's house in Suffolk.

The Glade stood beyond a quarry. We drove off the road, through gates topped with barbed wire, and followed a sandy track past great cranes, arrested, swinging silent in the wind until work would begin again on Monday. Yellow diggers perched dusty at the edge of deep pits, long rootling necks drooping like tulips. Brodie and Flook twisted their heads in fascination until the last scrap of rusted metal was lost from sight and we came to a green thicket, a tiny island marooned in the sandy desert. In the middle of the thicket was the Glade, a little house made big by the way Liza lived in it. We walked in through the Book Room. Even the ashtrays stood on stacks of books. More books spilled across the floor, covering the carpet, sliding, jostling, flapping their leaves in the draught, vying to be read.

Liza had a big round table in a room where you couldn't see out of the window because of the roses thrusting their way in. We children had supper and then wound through meandering paths in the garden to the Summer Palace, a concrete air-raid shelter transformed by Liza's green fingers into a tumbling scented bower of honeysuckle and wisteria. Inside the Summer Palace a television flickered on to a green leather sofa.

All Liza's children were there that weekend. Dominic had shed his suit and donned a pair of mud-encrusted boots, and was building a trellis outside the back door. 'Brodie, come and give me a hand,' he yelled when he saw us, and Brodie scrambled through a hedge to help him. Helen and Theresa sat with Mummy in the garden, glasses of green-white wine in their hands, shaded from the evening sun by decaying straw hats they had found heaped in the kitchen. They looked like three sisters, all pale-skinned, dark-haired and slender. Theresa's eyes were the same blue as Mummy's and she sat forward on her chair, gesturing with her hands to explain something just as Mummy always did. Helen leaned back and turned her face up to the sun. 'I'm so glad to be here again,' she said. 'I want to move back.'

Helen lived in Ireland and I had not seen her or her children for several years; Zoe and Vinnie were hard to recognize at first. Zoe was fifteen, her curling dark hair fell down her back and she looked like a gypsy princess with her gold hooped earrings and mass of clattering bracelets. I laughed when she said, 'Do you realize that even though I'm six months older than you, you are my aunt and so is Poppy?'

Vinnie, tongue-tied and confused by her ever-increasing family, stuck her thumb in her mouth and crouched on the grass at Helen's feet. 'Vinnie shouldn't suck her thumb,' whispered Dan. 'She's twelve, and when I was seven Mummy said mine would drop off if I went on sucking it.'

We closed the curtains in the Summer Palace so the grown-ups couldn't see Zoe and me smoking cigarettes. I pretended to inhale, the acrid smoke prickling my mouth.

Vinnie came in, a goldfish writhing and slipping on a wooden spoon in her hand. 'Fish soup tonight,' she giggled, and we ran out aghast. Around Liza's mossy pond little orange chips fluttered and flipped. Vinnie had scooped all the baby fish out of the water. We rescued them, our hands stroking the earth, trying to find every one in the gathering dusk.

In the house, Daddy and Liza stood talking at the fireplace. Music swooned from a pink tape recorder. Mummy was upstairs putting Dan and Poppy to bed. 'Is Liza your mother?' Dan asked her.

'No. She's Helen's mother.' Mummy tucked Poppy up and took Dan to brush his teeth. 'Liza's my friend and Daddy's friend.'

'How was Daddy old enough to have Helen and Dominic and Theresa?' Dan was determined to understand his family tree. I had been defeated trying to explain to him earlier. 'Ask Mummy. She told me,' I had suggested finally, exasperated by my lack of vocabulary for such complexities.

Zoe and I, Brodie, Vinnie and Flook were allowed to stay up later at Liza's than at home, and we played Scrabble in the kitchen, interrupted by shuffling adults.

Liza sat down with us, laying a blue packet of cigarettes and a glass in front of her. 'Can I play?' We gave her a space, but she wasn't concentrating, and she couldn't make a word. 'God, if I had the wits of you lot, I'd be a different creature, not half so scatty and hopeless,' she said, swaying into Zoe.

'Gran, you're not hopeless, don't be ridiculous,' said Zoe, and Liza leapt up, grabbed Flook and waltzed round the kitchen with him. 'They're always like this when they drink,' Brodie sighed.

'Your mother has tamed Patrick,' Liza gasped, prancing past the blackened stove, Flook gamely keeping up as they danced across the flagstones. 'She's saved him from himself. She is remarkable. I take my hat off to her. Do you?' Flook nodded, biting his lip, concentrating on steering Liza between sharp-edged objects. The rest of us decided to go to bed. Grown-ups drinking in their own room, being quiet and good, was one thing, but when they came and interrupted us, waffling drunkenly and interfering in our games, it was unbearable. Flook extracted himself and pounded up the stairs. We took off our shoes and climbed into bunk beds in the dormitory at the head of Liza's stairs. We were too tired to argue about who got the top bunks. Downstairs, the grown-ups were singing.

D aniel Auchoum was born the year Eleanor's parents left their house in Scotland. He was named Auchoum after it, and was all she had left of the place where she had grown up. Before the baby arrived, Va Va helped Eleanor fill a wicker basket with soft blankets. Arranging her favourite pink glass poodles around the cradle, Va Va prayed that this baby might be a girl. She yearned for a sister with ringlets and rosebud lips. Not a gun enthusiast, not a football-player, but someone to dress in frills like a giant doll. Someone of her very own.

She needed an ally. The nursery she still shared with Brodie and Flook offered no peace for her to read at night. Flook rolled from side to side for an hour after bedtime, droning 'Dilute to taste, dilute to taste', and Brodie built armies and flung them across the floorboards and into Va Va's no-man's-land bed. She turned her face to the wall and closed her eyes. When the girl baby came, everything would be different. There would be white socks and shiny buckled shoes next to a lacy cot. The guns and soldiers would retreat before swarms of dolls and handbags, earrings and hairslides, and Eleanor would call the Girls and the Boys in for supper, instead of the Boys and Va Va.

Patrick woke them early on a still summer morning. 'Darling hearts, you have a new baby brother.' Va Va burst into tears. Her mother had betrayed her, the infant had deceived her. Brodie and Flook bounced out of bed. 'Can we call him Pansy?'

Va Va sobbed. 'Daddy, we all wanted a girl baby. Are you sure we haven't got a girl?'

Patrick sat down. 'Angel, this tiny new baby needs you all to look after him. He's longing to meet his big brothers and sister. We can't make him unhappy with tears, can we?'

Dan came home from hospital a day later. He was big and placid, and he smiled straight away, flaunting his happiness in his new world. By the time he was six weeks old he slept through the night, his appetite was huge, and Va Va was reconciled to his maleness. He looked like a Renaissance cherub, sturdy, dimpled and golden. Eleanor called him Angel Delcare and basked in the radiant ease of his infancy. Va Va dragged him around by the neck and called him her baby.

Dan was a golden boy. Va Va, Brodie and Flook, uniformed in red boiler-suits like miniature Chinese workers, had big knees and long mud-daubed legs. Black hair tangled down their backs and their smiles were gap-toothed in filthy faces. Dan, round and brown, haloed with yellow curls, was their delight. He wore a red baseball cap rakishly askew and rolled on the lawn while Patrick lay reading beside him.

August 1988

Dan was almost seventeen when, one August Sunday, he rode a motorbike a hundred yards down the road to the pub. He hit a car and destroyed his future as an athlete. His right leg was smashed, the bone splintered into tiny pieces. He came home from hospital six weeks and seven operations later in a plaster cast. His leg, though damaged, was saved, but complications and fifteen further operations followed, and for years he limped a fine line between amputation and recovery.

I rang him in hospital the day after the accident, struggling to keep my voice steady as I listened to him. 'I hate it here. I want to go home. It hurts so much and I can't sleep. Everyone else here is old and one man just died in the bed across from me.' Dan sniffed, melancholy and alone.

I had not seen him yet and I could not imagine my tall, strong brother hemmed by plaster into a hospital bed. Dan had never stopped growing. He was still the baby of the family because he liked to be the baby, and Poppy wanted to be grown-up. He would perch on Mum's knee, cracking the chair and falling with her on to the kitchen floor, but every afternoon until his accident he trained for three hours with the Junior County football team. Dad was very proud of this. Mum struggled to scrape the money together for a specially made pair of football boots (Dan's feet were too big for regular ones), and Dan and Dad sat in the sun and got brown while discussing football tactics.

Dad insisted that he too had played top-class football, although Brodie and I, jealous of Dan and Dad's exclusive sport, doubted it. Stung by our scorn, Dad produced a photograph, small, sepia and crinkled, of young men with voluminous shorts and Charlie Chaplin smiles.

'Which is you?' But before Dad answered I saw Flook's face in the team. At nineteen they were identical, the same bones building the same features, more than fifty years apart.

Dan could never play again after his accident. His pride and his easy-going, happy nature made it impossible for the rest of us to see how much he minded. We guessed, and heaped guilt upon ourselves, secretly offering our own sound limbs to the gods in exchange for the return of Dan's. We had to make do with visiting him after his operations, bearing three Big Macs at a time. They vanished in seconds.

Poppy was a pale, delicate baby with the huge eyes of a hungry waif. Va Va was nine when her longed-for ally was born. Another girl. She was no longer the only girl. Now the boys had a sister who didn't boss them around and scream at them, but lay smiling dreamily as they played with her. Brodie and Flook, with two-year-old Dan trailing behind them, were a warrior tribe from which Va Va was excluded. She had not anticipated their interest in the new baby and was jealous of their doting glances at the cradle.

It was Easter when they first saw Poppy at the hospital. In the morning Va Va and her brothers loped round the garden, voices tossed away on the April breeze, collecting bright foil-covered rabbits left by the Easter Bunny. Gathering to compare booty, Va Va stiffened when Brodie announced, 'I'm going to take my second-best bunny to Poppy.' 'Yes. So am I,' said Flook, and they laid aside two red-wrapped rabbits.

Poppy lay like an amphibian exhibit in a glass box by Eleanor's bed. Blue veins meandered across her brow, her domed head bristled with fine hair, and Va Va felt sorry for her. She couldn't help being a girl. Va Va went home to make silver stars for

Poppy's bedroom ceiling. Her virtue suffered a setback when, planning to use the foil for a rainbow star, she went to look for her Easter eggs. On the windowsill the cosy cluster of fluffy chicks and bunnies had gone. In their place was a smear of chocolate carnage. Ripped foil tinkled in the draught and under the table Dobe chewed his toenail, dark eyes gleaming with guilt. 'How could you?' Va Va stamped her foot. 'This is all because we went to see the new baby. You're jealous of her, aren't you?' Va Va felt better; cleansed of her fury at the baby and martyred by the loss of her Easter eggs.

Poppy seemed a changeling child. Among her robust siblings she was like a china doll, white-skinned, hair peaking in a furry crest along her head. Her tapering fingers squelched in her food and she crowed with laughter as yoghurt dripped blotches on to the floor. Eleanor dressed her in lawn frocks and floral aprons and Poppy learnt to walk using Dobe as support. They left home together every morning, tripping down the drive to nowhere. Nervous of her apparent frailty, Va Va refrained from dragging her around by the neck as she had done with Dan.

As school manacled me ever more firmly to timetables and order and concentration, I began to rail against the lack of boundaries at home. Sitting on the bus beside Brodie's silent misery I watched the smear of car headlights quiver and flash past in the shrouded winter evening. Flook was spending the night with a friend. Brodie crouched in his blazer, his mottled knees poking from grey flannel shorts. His face was masked, half by the stiff collar abutting his chin, half by his loathed school cap. 'Why don't you take it off?' I asked.

'I can't bear even to touch it. You know, I'm supposed to raise it every time I see Mummy and Daddy or anyone else's parents or a master from school.' He shuddered, his voice hard and cold, small with dislike.

Brodie was good at games and excelled in his work, but he hated school. His intense shyness and wayward humour set him apart from his peers; he never mentioned any friends to us, far less brought them home. Mummy worried that he might be unpopular, and asked his form master. 'Archibald is an unsual boy' was all she got out of him. At home Brodie simmered on the Aga, reading, and hunted with his airgun through ploughed fields and clumps of woodland around the house. At night he slunk up to his attic bedroom to do his prep. He painted the attic black and daubed it with red gloss motifs copied from his shelf of books on Red Indians. He set his alarm clock for 3 a.m. so that he could wake, be conscious of the fact that it was not time for school, and slip back into luxurious slumber.

Mummy met us in Aylthorpe. She was late. We huddled by the bus-stop, shifting our feet to arrest the cold which gnawed the soles of our shoes and bit our bones. 'Who's at home?' I climbed over into the back through the only working door in the car. Brodie didn't speak; he drew a yellow exercise book from his satchel and began to mutter conjugations under his breath.

'Helen is back from Ireland, and she's brought a peculiar character called Rex. She's moving to Norwich.'

'Does that mean there won't be any supper?' Brodie scowled.

'Of course there's supper. We're having the rest of yesterday's corned beef hash.'

I sank down against an uncoiled spring in the back seat of the car and sighed. 'I hate Drinking Evenings.'

Our parents were poor. They had always been poor, and it had always been fine. We had animals and space and clothes and food; none of us was aware of money as a means towards anything but sweets on Saturday. But now Brodie, Flook and I were at school with children who lived in warm houses with carpets. Their fathers went out to work, and their mothers collected them from school in gleaming, silent cars which always worked. I led two lives, a day-time one of order and conformity followed by evenings of chaos.

Most of the time, the chaos was warm and familiar and comforting. In front of a bright fire, we sat with Mummy and read M.R. James ghost stories, or helped Daddy polish the old pewter jugs and tankards he picked up in junk shops along the coast. The thick walls of the house leaned inwards, welling heat, soporific and indulgent. Supper bubbled in the kitchen and the dogs yawned, curled like oversized shrimps in front of the hearth. Even going upstairs, through icy corridors where layer upon layer of cold heaped upon me until I reached the warm heart of my bedroom and the glow of the electric fire, was bearable.

But on Drinking Evenings the house smouldered angrily. The fire fizzed and belched smoke, no heat was given off by the wet logs. The kitchen cupboard sagged open, wafting a hint of old cheese and nothing else except some packets of lasagne corrugated by milk spilt long ago. The dogs scratched and the cats leapt on to the table, stealing anything, even raw potatoes, to express their anger. Brodie and I were clenched over our prep at the end of the kitchen table, ears closed crossly to the wine-stained voices of our parents and their friends. Upstairs, the corridor to our rooms was dark because the bulb had gone, and the chill air slapped my face as I hurried towards the snug haven of my room. But there the shock of cold was worse. My fire had not been turned on, and the little room lay forlorn, its private dignity struggling beneath neglect.

Helen sat next to us in the kitchen. She reeked of brandy, and her voice was deeper and more husky than usual, but her conversation thawed our frozen outrage. She was only five years younger than Mummy, but she never really seemed like a grown-up. Helen had almond-shaped eyes which flashed stone blue when she was angry, and her voice purred with the resonance of bass chords on a church organ. She drank too much for my teenage puritan taste, but I loved her mad bad stories and the wicked slant of her eyes when she laughed.

Long ago, Helen had met an old man on an aeroplane, and she bewitched him with her sorceress charms. When he died, he left her a legacy which took her and Zoe and Vinnie to Ireland. There the money slowly evaporated in a haze of whiskey and oysters, and the rent of a beautiful house. Helen returned to England, pregnant with her son and escorted by a musician called Rex. Rex's fingers were long, yellowed at the tips by nicotine, and his face was pitted and pale. He sat at our kitchen table drinking Guinness with whisky poured into it, silent until the spirits ignited his smouldering rage. Daddy tried to talk to him, but became angry and went to bed. From my room above the kitchen I heard the house go quiet, and I fell asleep. Hours later, the still night was broken by crashing doors.

'You are the devil's whore!' Rex screeched at Helen in the room below my bedroom. I shivered in my warm bed and hid my head under the quilt. I listened breathless for a scream or a thump. There was nothing, and in the morning, Rex and Helen sat at breakfast unscathed.

Feeding the new batch of hens, I glanced covetously at Zoe's pink leg-warmers. She and Vinnie had missed the beginning of term, and they were not going to school until after Christmas. This was also enviable. We finished feeding the hens and went up to my room. Vinnie leaned towards the dusty mirror and plaited her hair into tiny braids while Zoe and I sat on the bed

96

and she told me about Ireland. 'Mum took us to a fair there. There were gypsy caravans and fiddlers. We stayed for three days, and we had to sleep in a tent.' Zoe twisted the silver rings on her fingers as she talked and puffed expertly on a cigarette she had stolen from her mother's bag.

'Zoe had a boyfriend in Ireland,' said Vinnie, her wide smile the only part of her reflection visible through the decay of my mirror. Zoe, smoking, wearing make-up and carrying a handbag, seemed almost grown-up. Helen confided in her as an equal, and between them they looked after twelve-year-old Vinnie, sharing the responsibility of clean clothes, food and attendance at school.

Helen loved her daughters, but she was sometimes ill, and often depressed. She and Zoe argued and made up, while Vinnie bottled up her feelings and escaped to ride ponies whenever she could. I knew that they had different fathers, and that Vinnie's had been a West Indian musician. Camouflaged in the safety of two parents, I pretended not to notice that they never mentioned their fathers. I didn't know if they even knew them. I took Vinnie riding, and Zoe read a story to Poppy. She was looking forward to Helen's new baby. They stayed for the weekend and then drove off in Rex's grey van to the new house Helen had rented in Norwich.

Patrick's sixtieth birthday was commemorated by a book, and his party was written up by three newspapers. Va Va, Brodie and Flook thought they had become famous when they saw their photographs in the papers. 'What a pity Dan and Poppy were asleep,' said Va Va piously, having made certain there was no mention of them in any of the articles.

Trixie, generously extending her godmotherly role to the whole family, gave Patrick's party in London. She and her silent husband Russell lived in a house as white as icing, with great stone steps leading up to the front door. Eleanor and Patrick paused in the hall and a brace of ladies with white aprons took their coats and whisked Dan and Poppy upstairs.

In the blood-red dining-room more white-aproned women milled, arranging glasses and prinking canapés. Overawed, Va Va, Brodie and Flook followed their parents through the echoing house and upstairs to get ready.

Trixie summoned Eleanor to her room, Va Va followed. Clothes lolled everywhere, a pile of them wrapped in transparent polythene gleamed and rustled on the bed. 'Eleanor, choose something, choose anything,' boomed Trixie, embracing her.

'I've brought my blue velvet dress, I think I'll wear that,' said Eleanor, blinking at the array.

Trixie's eyes sagged at the corners. 'Won't you just try this lilac one?' she urged, raising a froth of purple lace. Her shirt, straining across her jutting bosom, suddenly drooped as a button spun off and fell, lost in the thick pile of the carpet. Va Va giggled and was sent up yet more stairs to dress herself. Buoyed up with excitement, Brodie and Flook flung pillows across the bedroom. Va Va cajoled Brodie into trying on her lime-green nylon nightie, smuggled into her suitcase when Eleanor was not looking. Eleanor entered, a princess from Hans Christian Andersen in a sweeping gown of silk velvet the colour of her eyes. Purple earrings quivered behind strands of hair and she smelt of summer.

'Brodie, take that thing off. Va Va, I told you not to bring it. Now will you hurry up and get dressed.' The children flung off their jeans and jerseys and, in seconds, Brodie and Flook were dressed in matching navy shirts and red trousers. Va Va slouched on the bed; she wanted to wear her lime-green nightie. Patrick had brought it back for her from America and it was her favourite dress. Eleanor loathed it, and paid Va Va not to wear it to children's parties at home. But today there was no alternative: Va Va had not brought another dress. Skipping with joy, she entered the drawing-room with Eleanor, nylon wafting softly as she moved.

'Darlings, you look beautiful,' said Patrick, raising his glass in a toast to them.

People arrived and arrived, none seemed to leave and the house swelled and hummed with talk. Squeezing through to find Patrick, Va Va scratched her ear on a button and submitted to spattering kisses. 'My, haven't you grown? You must be ten now, Gabriella. How is your baby sister? You won't remember me, I came to Mildney last summer.' Women with painted faces purred at her and smiled. She couldn't find Patrick anywhere, or Brodie or Flook.

Eleanor came down the stairs. 'I've been to see Dan and Poppy. They're both sound asleep and Mrs Damley is watching them.'

A man with red hair and a broad Scottish accent came up. 'Eleanor, you look like a goddess.' He squinted down at Va Va. 'Hello, young lady. I'm Angus Dean. Have you heard of me?' Va Va backed towards her mother and shook her head. 'I'm a Catholic homosexual orphan from Glasgow. Your father is a very famous, very brilliant poet. I hope you're proud of him.'

Va Va glared at the man, suspicion freezing her scowl. 'You're too old to be an orphan,' she said, but he wasn't listening.

'I'll take you to Trixie's room and you can watch television,' said Eleanor and led her up the stairs.

'What's a homosexual?' Va Va asked as they threaded past more people on the landing.

'I'll tell you some other time,' replied Eleanor.

Brodie and Flook were cocooned in Trixie's mighty bed, sausage rolls strewn at their feet. Va Va climbed in between them and *Kojak* began.

October 1988

Trixie divorced Russell and came to stay at Mildney with her new boyfriend, David. We were all there for the weekend. On Saturday morning David put on a builder's helmet and a checked shirt and went out with his chainsaw to cut up fallen trees in the Wilderness. Trixie, her hair held back by a child's pink hairband adorned with two bobbing antennae, stamped round the house waking us all up. 'Come on, you lot, I want to talk to you. Present yourselves in the playroom in ten minutes.'

Groaning, I turned over, burying my face in the pillow, but Trixie was not to be defeated. Into my room she thumped, the yellow fluff-balls on the ends of her antennae swivelling as they brushed the ceiling. 'You can marshal your brothers, Va Va.' She sounded like a drill-sergeant chivvying soldiers on parade. I got up.

There was a tray of tea in the playroom. I poured five mugfuls and handed them to the others as they slouched in; hair tangled from sleep, jerseys inside out. Brodie had holes in the toes of his socks; rosy flesh peeped rudely from grey wool as he sat down.

Trixie enjoyed being in command. Her visits to Mildney were infrequent, but whenever she came her mission was to change things. Mum was fond of her, but she never failed to upset someone with her two-pronged approach of generosity and bullying. She bought Mum a new washing machine and then policed it, banning any items of clothing belonging to the boys. 'They can use a laundrette,' she insisted. 'Their ghastly jeans will break it immediately, and as for their socks . . .' She paused, dragged on her cigarette and exhaled a frill of blue smoke from her nose. 'My dear, they should be incinerated.'

In the playroom Trixie slumped her bulk on to the arm of a chair. She gazed round at all of us, eyes wide, face pulled into sensitive mode.

'Now I want you all to listen to me. I have spoken to your mother, and although she never complains – dear Eleanor, she is a saint – I know she is desperately worried about money.'

Flook sighed and got up to refill his mug. He frowned into the fireplace. 'Why isn't Mum involved in this conversation?' he asked.

Trixie blinked several times. 'She's too embarrassed, act-ually.' She sighed. 'She's hiding in the loo, if you must know.' Trixie laughed and looked round at us expectantly. None of us responded. She continued, 'Anyway. It's time you all helped your parents a bit. They've helped you, and now you are grown-up and earning money you can afford to let go of the selfishness of youth.'

Dan and Poppy hissed venom towards her and she acknowl-edged them with a nod. 'You two could give up your pocket-money and stop scrounging cigarettes, but I know you aren't earning. And of course Dan's leg is a dreadful worry for her.'

'It's not much fun for me either,' said Dan.

Trixie coughed. 'Va Va, Brodie and Flook can each give ten pounds a week.'

There was a long silence. Brodie stared at Trixie, his gaze steady, forcing her to look back at him. She lowered her eyes. 'I know you think I shouldn't interfere, but I don't care, it has to be said.'

I couldn't decide if I hated her more for her ham-fisted approach or for being right. Anyway, I hated her.

'Thank you for your lecture.' Brodie walked towards the door. 'I'm going to talk to Mum about it. We will do what she wants us to, *not* what you tell us to.' He paused before leaving the room. 'And why are you wearing that ridiculous thing on your head?'

Trixie reached up and felt her drooping antennae. She gasped and laughed, eyes snapping shut, mouth gaping wide as hilarity bowled through her. Silent, treading softly, curving round her like cats shrinking from water, we all left the room.

Mum was crying in the kitchen. 'I told her not to. I begged her not to,' she wept, 'but Trixie insisted. I am sorry, all of you. Just ignore her.'

Hooting guffaws still issued from the playroom. Brodie shut the door. 'Mum, you should have told us. We don't mind. It's just being told by her.'

Mum blew her nose. 'Well, every little helps,' she managed to say.

Eleanor cured Patrick of drinking whisky. When she met him he would start and finish a bottle in an evening. By surreptitiously pouring half of each new bottle down the lavatory and topping it up with water, she weaned him from this dangerous nectar and steered him into a routine where he only drank on Saturdays.

Red Martini, spiced and sickly, was his next peccadillo. He would clasp the bottle by the neck and keep it close to him all evening, challenging anyone who tried to share it.

Patrick rarely invited the children into the Drinking Room. It was like a museum, deep shelves, deep dust, icons and a Chinese pipe. His special things. Patrick loved ritual, and he lit the fire in the Drinking Room at five o'clock on Saturday evenings. Then he went upstairs and had a bath, returning in clean clothes but the same scuffed cowboy boots, like a priest ready for Mass. He stood at the mantelpiece with his first glass of wine, head to one side listening to the opening melody of every Saturday night; the babbling summer notes of Theodorakis's 'On the Beach' issued from the gramophone, heralding another Drinking Evening.

Va Va was eight when she was invited, one afternoon, to help

Patrick rearrange his Drinking Room things. Reaching back on a shelf for the broken wing of a plaster cherub, she found a tiny box of books. Eight bruised purple covers in miniature. 'I shall give you these on your fifteenth birthday,' said Patrick. Va Va shivered in the shadow of future sophistication. Something in the Drinking Room was hers.

At school on Monday, all the sleek, shiny-haired girls with freshly ironed shirts and polished shoes discussed their neat, comfortable weekends, and I felt a thousand miles from home. It was nearly my birthday, and my friends wanted to know how it was to be celebrated.

'Mummy and Daddy are taking me to the theatre and out to supper,' I lied breezily. 'And for my present I'm going to have my ears pierced.'

'Dilly had her ears pieced and a party dress,' said someone, and I found myself responding, 'Oh yes. Mummy's having one made for me already.'

My fifteenth birthday dawned with decadence. Daddy was to drive us to school so that the family tradition of birthday presents at breakfast could be conducted at a reasonable hour rather than five in the morning. I had the ritualistic card-opening and was gratefully surprised to receive a cheque for five pounds from my grandparents. One envelope came covered in mud. It had no stamp, just my name scrawled badly across the top left-hand corner. Inside was a lilac-and-pink cut-out ballerina from Mr Cardew's, with loving scratches, paw marks and wobbling crosses (the signatures of those unable to write) from all the animals. Shalimar, with typical ostentation, had used a lump of coal to sign his name, and it came off all over my hands and my pale school jersey.

I did not expect any presents because I was to have my ears pierced after school that afternoon, but in the tiled arches under the kitchen window a pile of lumpy, shiny parcels awaited me. Daddy sat with Poppy at the end of the table, posting jammy squares of toast into her round mouth. Mummy cleared a space among the bowls and plates, insisting on wiping the table before the presents were opened. 'Come on, Ellie, let's see what Va Va's got.' Daddy was excited; he loved presents, and opened his own impatiently, all at once, losing small things beneath a foam of ripped wrapping. 'All right. I'm just coming.' Mummy wiped her hands, lobster-red and veined from washing-up, down her skirt, and reached for the first parcel. 'This is to Va Va with much love from Daddy,' she read, and the kitchen fell silent apart from the ticking of the clock. I opened a small, heavy parcel, tearing the silver foil which Daddy always used to wrap his presents. It was the set of books from the Drinking Room, the books he had promised me years ago, and which I had forgotten entirely. 'My Own Library' read the faded gold script engraved across the green leather pediment framing the books. 'Oh Daddy, thank you.' I squeezed past chairs to kiss him. 'I can't believe you remembered about these books.' 'Neither can I.' Mummy looked amazed. Daddy smiled slowly. 'They mark a turning-point, my love. You are no longer a child.'

My next present was from Dan. It was a red rubber moustache. I put it on and Flook laughed so much that he forgot about his porridge, and sank his chin into it. A purse, some bathsalts and some books from Brodie and Flook followed, and then a nearly clean handkerchief from Poppy. 'I bought it from Mr Cardew with my pocket money for you, and I tried it out on the way home. It does work, I promise.'

'To darling Va Va, with love from Mummy,' Mummy read out on the last parcel. 'You can take it back if you don't like it. I asked the woman in the shop,' she said, before I had begun to open it. Pink teddy-bear paper fell away, revealing a smooth pillow of palest cream silk. I lifted a corner. Loosened from its tissue paper, a dress cascaded towards the floor, soft as a rose petal with lace foaming in hoops around the skirt. Mummy looked anxious as I held it up against myself, craning her neck to see my expression, hidden by hair. 'It's old,' she said. 'Twenties, I think, but I thought it would really suit you, darling.' Then, nervously, 'Do you like it?' I looked up, radiant. 'Wow,' was all I could say. There was a sudden rush as Flook realized it was nearly eight o'clock, and time to leave for school. I regained the faculty of speech enough to thank Mummy and Daddy, and drove to school numb with pleasure, anticipating the jealous disbelief of my school friends. We were even going to the theatre, although Daddy had refused to come, stating piously, 'The bambini need looking after.' Brodie said he would come instead.

After school, I hurried the mile between school and Jones's, where I was to have my ears pierced. Square grey houses loomed from belts of spruce, televisions flickering in downstairs rooms. Street-lights flared in the creeping dusk as I walked and I was glad to reach the crowded High Street. In Jones's I pushed my hood down and a cold prickle of sweat rushed over me as hot air steamed out of knee-high heaters. I dawdled on the ground floor, wondering which tights would look best with my new dress. I chose a sparkling pair, and earmarked them for when Daddy had cashed my cheque for me. In the lift I pressed the button for the third floor, and the beauty salon. The lift was small. Just as the doors were closing, a man dashed in and stood behind me. Floating up to the third floor, I was disturbed by wafts of alcohol. I got out and idled by some stationery. I wondered what kind of birthday cake Mummy had made, and if I would be allowed a glass of wine now I was fifteen. The man from the lift was beside me, his red-rimmed eyes watery, staring into mine. His grey coat was undone, hands clasped through his pockets in front of him. He panted heavily, alcohol bitter on his breath. Over the collar of his coat, wispy fair hair drooped from a loose pony-tail. Mesmerized, like a rabbit in headlights, I stared back, curdling with cold fear. He was not very old.

He spoke low and fast, obscene in his urgent need to communicate. 'I've seen you. I've been watching you every day.' Bile, salty, suffocating, rose in my throat, and my knees shook. I could not drag my eyes away. 'You go to Mary Hall,' he continued. 'You are different from the others. I know you, I know your name. I see all the girls, but you are the best. I want you to come with me now.'

His voice, his grotesque words, his stinking presence, overwhelmed me for what seemed like hours. I wanted to scream, but I couldn't find the right signals. Suddenly I did; paralysis left me. I ran, hurling myself at the nearest cashier. The man loped away down the emergency stairs. Now I had found my voice I couldn't stop screaming, clutching the cash lady, shaking until I ached. She led me into a little office, but I wouldn't let her leave me there in case the man came back. A phone rang, and she answered it. 'It's all right, love, they've caught him downstairs. Someone saw him following you into the shop, and had already told the detectives. He's with the police now.' She came and sat next to me, hugging me and stroking my arm. 'Let's phone your mum, shall we?' I nodded and told her the number. I sat in silence, tears pouring down my face. He had followed me. He had followed me. What did he want to do to me? I wasn't different. I was like everybody else at school. Why had he picked me? Was it my fault?

A girl at school had been raped, we had been told one morning in assembly. We must be careful. I had listened and felt pity for the unnamed girl, but although I walked briskly down the street, I never imagined being followed or accosted, or raped. I didn't know what rape was. It sounded like something to do with a sword. Had I now been raped? It was shaming; I blushed crimson, embarrassment breaking over waves of shock. Mummy and Daddy arrived, and a policeman came in and asked me what the man had said. Another policeman stood to one side with Daddy and the man who had raised the alarm. I heard one of them say in an undertone, 'We've sent men into his flat. They've found photographs of the girls coming home from school, hundreds of them. And others, worse, much worse. He's a nutcase. Thank God he's done no harm to your daughter.'

'It's my birthday, my birthday,' I sobbed as we drove home, and Mummy rocked me in her arms. Daddy vented his anger by driving like an Italian all the way home. For once, Mummy didn't even flinch.

A few days later, the nice man who had noticed the pervert sent me a book token. 'Jones's sent me this,' he wrote, 'but I think you need it more than I do. I hope you are feeling better now, and that you can forget your horrible experience.'

I did not forget it, but it sank to the bottom of my mind as Christmas and the holidays approached. I had been invited to a dance by a girl called Imogen Lyttleton-Fraser. Daddy and the boys teased me about the smart party, and Daddy called her 'Ima Little Freezer', but I paid no attention. Mummy and I discussed my clothes exhaustively.

'I'll wear my new dress of course, and those sparkling tights, but I don't have any shoes except the red velvet ones you gave me. I know, I'll paint them gold.'

'And what about your hair? Some combs might be nice.' Mummy was making sausage rolls, her arms a blur of bright white where the flour had stuck to them like long, soft gloves. Dan came running into the kitchen, knees muddy, face pink from football training. He grabbed a sausage roll. Mummy screamed, 'They aren't cooked, you'll get worms!' but he had already swallowed it whole. 'That'll teach you,' I said sourly. Dan groaned and ran out again. We heard retching sounds from the yard.

On the day of the party I spent all afternoon getting ready. Lingering in the bath, I submerged every angle of my bony knees, hips and shoulders in the fog of water as the bathroom evaporated in steam. Everything had to be just right.

A newly-washed towel from the airing cupboard, holey and singed, a faint aroma of bacon drifting from it; a new bottle of shampoo, bought specially, and a capful of rare bluebell bath essence given to Mummy for her birthday. My bedroom was warm, scented with joss sticks like a church heavy with incense before Mass. I put a pile of records on to my newly-acquired gramophone and danced around, hoping that this was the sort of thing other girls did before parties. Beads and ornaments clinked on their shelves and the little room shook. I saw myself dancing in the mirror. I narrowed my eyes, imagining I was Cleopatra in my brown towel, my long hair, never thick enough to make a decent pony-tail, draped wet across my shoulders. I dressed, not as languorously as I had hoped. Goose-bumps stippled my flesh, and I fell over sideways on the bed trying to pull my new sparkling tights over damp legs. Once the dress was on, I leant towards the mirror and dabbed my eyelids with some mole-brown eyeshadow Mummy had given me. Spitting into an old cake of mascara, a trophy from a visitor's handbag, I scrubbed the little brush through the puddle. The spiky effect on my eyelashes was most satisfactory. I had to climb on to the bed and then bend double to see my whole body, but I liked the contorted result. I went downstairs to show Mummy and Daddy.

Daddy was reading by the fire. He looked round, then stood up and reached out his arms to me. 'Beautiful, my love. What exquisite taste you and your Mummy have. That dress is marvellous.' And he called through to Mummy, who was reading to Dan in the playroom, 'Eleanor. Come and look at this

112

beautiful daughter of ours.' Half embarrassed, half delighted, I pirouetted in front of the fire.

The heater in the car was broken. I put on a stiff sheepskin coat I found in the back and wiggled my toes to keep them from dropping off. We drove slowly. Specks of snow melted on the windscreen and were replaced by furred flakes fluttering like moths in the headlights. The car slid down a drive lit on both sides by guttering beacons. Imogen's house rose spectral in front of us. The front door was open, a Christmas tree twinkled within, and white fairy-lights studded the creepers which grew up the front of the house.

'Look Daddy, isn't it lovely?' I gasped, quivering with pre-party nerves.

Daddy kissed me. 'Have a wonderful time, my love. And make sure someone has a decent pumpkin to bring you home in.'

We laughed, and he drove off as I stepped into the hall. Imogen was there. She looked very like the fairy twinkling at the top of the two-storey Christmas tree. 'I say, Gabriella, what a gorgeous dress,' she said, when I removed my sheepskin coat. 'Put that thing upstairs and then come through.'

I glided up the wide shallow steps, looking forward to coming down them again like Scarlett O'Hara, and breathed the heavy, oily scent of pine mingling with candle wax. I hadn't seen anyone I knew yet, but my head was so filled with dreams that I would have found it hard to cope with a real human being. In a tall bedroom I found a throng of giggling girls from school putting on lipstick in front of the mirror. They were all wearing pretty dresses with bows at their necks and sashes at their waists. They fell silent and smirked when they saw me. 'Gosh. Look at your dress,' said a blancmange-pink one, 'it's very grown-up, isn't it?' I looked through the group of bell skirts and tight bodices to my own reflection in the long mirror, and my hazy dreams shrivelled to dust. In my high heels, carefully gilded with a spray can of car paint, I towered above them. My dress had tiny straps of lace, and my flesh looked sinful and naked beside their puffed organdie sleeves and velvet bows. I saw my hands, huge and blue with cold. They looked like hams. I did not know what to do with them, so I crossed my arms. I wanted to go home.

Downstairs went the rustling twitter of schoolgirls. I followed them slowly, hoping I wouldn't overbalance but determined not to uncross my arms and reveal my hands. I forgot about being Scarlett O'Hara. Imogen's parents were with her in the hall, her mother tiny, with the fragile face of a doe and a thin smile, her father bluff and genial. 'Do go through and have some punch, dear,' said Imogen's mother. 'Are you cold?' I shook my head miserably, taking her remark as criticism of my flimsy dress, and stumbled through into a darker room. Music boomed from a black box in the corner, masterminded by a boy in dirty jeans and a paint-spattered shirt.

Sasha Warton was there, and I joined her, grateful to be disguised a little by her height. She too was wearing puffed sleeves and bows, but she looked at my dress with real envy, and I felt better. Before us squatted a vast stone fireplace, its heart blazing with tree trunks. On the walls, gilt-framed paintings of men in wigs and women with powdered ringlets peeped from a hedge of holly.

Someone gave me a glass of punch; it tasted of lemonade,

and I drank it in one nervous gulp. Sasha passed me a purple cigarette with a gold tip, and I coughed as she lit it for me. 'Don't swallow the smoke,' she said, watching me gulp and then choke, 'Try to breathe it in.' I tried, and swooning dizziness followed a rush of nausea.

I peered around the room; there were boys everywhere. Most of them were smaller than I was. Sasha was talking to a medium-sized boy called James. I wondered what she could be saying to him, and was listening, my eyes half shut in concentration, when someone touched my arm. I jumped and turned round. It was a very short boy, with an astonishingly deep voice. 'Hello, I'm Imogen's cousin Tim,' he said. 'Will you come and dance?' Amazed, I nodded. He led me on to the dance floor and whisked me around very fast. I had been to one or two discos with my brothers. We usually stood around the edge and watched other people dancing. I had never danced with a boy before, and did not feel ready for the experience. Tim had great determination, and after a minute of elephantine galumphing into people and tripping over, I began to enjoy myself.

Tim had evidently been made master of ceremonies by his aunt. What Tim did, everyone did. After our dance, two other boys, one large, one medium, asked me to dance, and then another large one. I had escaped into fantasy, and the last one looked to me like Rhett Butler. I felt popular and beautiful, and fancied myself as the belle of the ball. Forgotten was my wickedly exposed flesh.

'My name is James Merry-Curl,' he said.

I snorted with laughter. 'Sorry, sorry. It's just that it's a funny name,' I said, noticing his hurt expression.

'Your name is pretty funny too,' he pointed out. 'Everyone says your parents are really weird. Are they hippies?'

I glared at him. 'They are not weird, and they're not hippies. Who says they are, anyway?'

Merry-Curl reddened, his film-star glamour disappearing for ever. 'Oh, you know. Imogen and the other girls. They say that your parents are really poor and that you've got twenty-five brothers and sisters and you live in some weird place like a gypsy's house.'

He was now so embarrassed that he couldn't stop, and I listened in silence, my whole body tensed in humiliation and anger. 'How old are you?' I asked him.

'Eighteen,' he said, miserably shifting, dying to get away.

'Can you drive?'

'Yes, why?'

'Well, you can take me away from this hateful party and drive me home. Then you can see for yourself what my family is like, as you seem so interested.'

Merry-Curl's pink cheeks blenched, and his eyes bulged with horror. 'Oh, God. Umm, I'm awfully sorry, but I don't think I can. I have to take my sister back home, you see.'

Angry and trapped, exposed by two-faced schoolgirls and their feeble-minded consorts, I wanted to go home. I had longed to be like them and liked by them, and they had conspired against me. Merry-Curl mumbled something about getting a drink, and attempted a smile before moving away from me backwards. I watched with a flicker of satisfaction as he bumped into Imogen's mother, spilling her drink over her wrist. I looked around for Sasha, but she was dancing, her arms and legs swaying like branches. Her sister Annie came over to me, her boyfriend clamped to her side as he had been all evening. Annie was older and more worldly than the other girls at the party, and Chris, her boyfriend, looked like a pop star in his glittering yellow and green striped jacket. Annie wore a black rubber dress and her legs were enmeshed in fishnet tights. Black kohl rimmed her eyes, and her face was unnaturally pale. No one else there had a boyfriend.

'This is so dire,' she sighed, leaning against the wall next to me and taking a sip of my drink. 'Let's go. Do you want to come with us, Gabriella?' Annie had never spoken to me before, and now she was inviting me to escape with her. I nodded eagerly, she fastened me to the boyfriend-free side of her wiggling rubber body, and we moved out into the hall.

Merry-Curl was sitting on a radiator with Alice Grey, a girl in the year above me at school, perched on his knee. They both looked very uncomfortable. Alice's legs were braced against the floor so Merry-Curl would think she was less heavy than she was. His face was obscured by her hair, and his hands drooped uselessly by his side. Alice gazed at the wall above Merry-Curl's head. She looked awkward and too big, not like Poppy snuggled on Mummy's lap, more a gormless cuckoo trying to be a tiny lark. I smirked and ran upstairs for my coat.

Chris's car had only two seats. It was a mini pick-up truck, and I had to hover in the gap above the handbrake as we drove. Annie had decided to take me home, and as Chris never spoke, he could not disagree.

'Will your parents be up? Will your father be reading poetry? Will any of your brothers be there? Will there be a fight?'

Annie was annoying me. I was not being taken home because she liked me, but because she wanted to meet my father. 'They're not like that,' I said impatiently. 'They're perfectly normal.'

We drew up outside Mildney, and I noticed with a sinking heart that there were several cars parked behind the house. It was a Drinking Evening.

There were always people at Mildney, and many of them were Fans, Poetry Fans. First they wrote, then they telephoned, then they came, eager to pay homage to The Poet. Patrick would only tolerate them on Saturdays. Brodie, Flook and Va Va founded a kingdom beyond the river with three islands named Fuck, Shit and Hell. The names were part of their sinful secrecy. Springing out from the reeds around their domain, the children greeted cars crawling up the drive, a phalanx of mud-coated outriders brandishing sticks and home-made guns.

Newcomers were nervous and indulgent, poised to greet the children. The American ones brought presents, the German ones came on motorbikes. Va Va fiddled with her hair, legs twisted coyly, when Eleanor said, 'And this is Gabriella, but we call her Va Va.' It was the handbags, not the guests, which were interesting. Va Va had two of her own, identical, shiny, one pink, one blue, given on the same birthday by Eleanor and Granny. She spied a bulging green one near a chair and sidled over. 'Can I play with your handbag?' The woman laughed. 'Of course, why not?' Va Va knelt down and lost herself in the musty leather folds of someone else's life.

Eleanor did not have much make-up, and what she did have was hers and not for playing with, Va Va had been told a thousand times. But a stranger, wanting to make friends, was more forthcoming. Out came scent, exotic in a round bottle with a gold stopper, breathing a hint of the delectable promise inside. Out came lipstick, heavy in a bullet-shaped tube and tasting of violets and Vaseline. Out came a purse, jangling with coins. One would be given to Va Va. She paraded it in front of Brodie. ''S' not fair,' he whined to Patrick, who leaned forward to hear him, then reached into his pocket for a sixpence.

Children's supper was haphazard. People milled in the kitchen – 'Eleanor, do let me help' – and then stood smoking, talking, talking, talking, while Eleanor spooned baked beans and yoghurt into anyone within reach. No toothbrushing or face-washing on Drinking Evenings. Straight upstairs. Brodie built a castle on his bed. Sheets thrust over the spikes where he had unscrewed his bed knobs made a canopy beneath which he sat cross-legged, smirking. Flook and Va Va copied him. Three castles, three pairs of ripped sheets, toys catapulting across the wasteland of the room and bombing against the castle walls.

Va Va went on a mission for provisions at half-time. The kitchen was empty, plates strewn across the table, festooned spaghetti, half-eaten, hanging from them. All the grown-ups were in the Drinking Room, forbidden territory on Saturday nights. Through a crack in the door Va Va could see a bright sliver of flame reflected in the glass of the french windows and Patrick leaning one arm upon the mantelpiece.

He didn't see her when she sidled in to whisper something to Eleanor. He stood close to a man, talking. Abruptly he moved back, smashing his glass into the fire. 'I beseech you in the bowels of Christ to remove this interloper.' The man edged towards the door, someone else filled the space at Patrick's side. Patrick frowned. 'Eleanor. Read me something beautiful,' he growled, and her low voice fell into the silent room:

> 'The sigh that heaves the grasses
>> Whence thou wilt never rise
> Is of the air that passes
>> And knows not if it sighs.

> 'The diamond tears adorning
>> Thy low mound on the lea,
> Those are the tears of morning,
>> That weeps, but not for thee.'

Va Va hung around at the top of the stairs, peering through the banisters. A fat man lurched into the hall. He opened the front door and peed noisily and long into the garden. Va Va clenched her fists around the banisters and scowled. 'How dare he? We don't even know him.'

Liza's son Dominic, Va Va's half-brother, shuffled ponderous and sideways out of the Drinking Room; his face was puffy and sentimental with drink. 'You should be in bed, Gabriella, this is grown-ups' time.' He raised his glass to his lips and crashed headlong to the floor. Va Va held her breath, waiting for someone to come. The Drinking Room was loud with laughter.

No one came. She tiptoed down the stairs. Dominic smelt stale and boozy, his nose was pleated red against the tiles. He was breathing. 'Not dead,' she thought. 'It serves him right.'

Now Patrick was singing, his empty glass a microphone held under his chin. Va Va's eyes pinched with tiredness; she longed for them all to go to bed, to go away and make the house safe again. She sat on the stairs and listened.

> 'The train don't stay love
> It goes straight through
> And now it's gone love
> And so are you
>
> 'Build me a castle
> Forty feet high
> So I can see her
> As she goes by
>
> 'Bird in a cage love
> Bird in a cage
> Dying for freedom
> Ever a slave.'

Annie unwound herself from the pick-up truck, shivering in her thin dress, and followed me into the house.

'I say, it's Cinderella back from the ball.' Daddy's elbows were on either side of a plate of food. Twisted cigarette butts protruded from mashed potato like crippled seedlings. 'How nice of you to come home.' He turned to the man sitting next to him. 'My daughter moves in the most exalted circles these days,' he drawled. 'She is becoming a member of the upper classes and wishes to forget her poverty-stricken family.'

'You're drunk, Daddy. Don't be foul.' My voice wobbled. 'What's wrong with my friends anyway? You sent me to that school, and that's where I met them.'

Mummy intervened. 'Pay no attention. He's been perfectly ghastly all evening. He's bored and he's secretly dying to hear about your party.'

'Darling heart, come and tell me some lies.' Daddy was smiling now, reaching his hand out to me.

'Are you going to be nice?' I squeezed past a red-nosed woman on his right. The man opposite stood up, a pipe swinging on his lip, and shook hands with me. 'Victor Schmidt,'

123

he said, and gestured to the red-nosed woman, 'and this is my wife, Evelyn.' Evelyn sniffed.

Daddy sneered, narrowing his eyes, 'Evelyn is a practising lesbian. Her conversation is superfluous until she admits this.'

Evelyn shrank away from him and burst into tears, dabbing at her nose with a frilly handkerchief.

'Patrick, for heaven's sake leave her alone.'

Evelyn wailed and rushed from the room. Daddy slammed the table with his glass. 'I will not tolerate hypocritical little bitches in my house,' he yelled. Victor took a swig from a bottle of red wine and looked up at the ceiling. Mummy disappeared to find Evelyn, and Annie, eyes starting from her head in glee, wriggled past Evelyn's upturned chair and sat down next to Daddy.

'Who the hell are you?'

'Daddy, this is Annie, Sasha's sister. She brought me home from the party.'

Daddy raised his glass to Chris. 'You must be the pumpkin then, dear boy,' he said. Chris cowered by the Aga, a protective shield of cat curved in his arms. He blushed and nodded. Annie lit a cigarette and swivelled herself nearer to Daddy. He looked at her, a smile glimmering. 'You look like a hooker,' he said. Annie simpered and said primly, 'Thank you.'

Daddy laughed and passed her a yellow mug. 'Here, have a drink.' He poured wine into the bottom of the mug, then topped it up with water. 'This is how we get drunk in Italy, dear heart. Intoxication should be gradual.'

Weak with relief, I leaned next to Chris, keeping a good distance from the table. I found a box of chocolates melting in the top oven and in silence Chris and I consumed them.

Annie bombarded Daddy with questions. His mood had changed. 'You are impertinent,' he said gently, when she asked, 'How did you get to be a poet?' But he liked her, and even Victor unbent a little from his umbrage when Daddy took his glass like a microphone and sang 'My Snowy-Breasted Pearl'. Evelyn did not return; Victor was so drunk that he failed to notice her absence when he went to bed. The phone rang very late. Daddy had gone to bed; Annie and Chris, she wreathed in smiles, he in yawns, had departed, promising to come back soon. It was Evelyn. In the village telephone-box.

'I am taking a taxi to Norwich where I shall spend the night in a hotel. The taxi is collecting me from the churchyard. Please could you tell Victor to meet me at the Maid's Head tomorrow morning.'

Mummy pleaded with Evelyn to return but she would have none of it. 'I shall never set foot in that house again, Eleanor.'

Mummy came back into the kitchen. 'I'd better go and wake Victor,' she said, 'Evelyn is in a terrible state.'

Victor refused to do anything, so Mummy gave up and kissed me goodnight. 'Darling, I haven't heard a word about your party yet. You must tell me it all tomorrow.'

Christmas 1988

For the first time, we did not all come home for Christmas. Flook was away, hitch-hiking across America. He sent frequent postcards offering glimpses of his adventures.

'*New York*. Robbed on the subway – lost everything except my money and my life.'

'*Salt Lake City*. Met a pretty girl and followed her in through a big door. She slammed it, it was a Mormon Church – narrow escape.'

'*Big Sur*. Stood on a cliff drinking orange juice at dawn and saw a school of whales heading south. May follow them.'

Mum was neurotic for three days after each of these postcards arrived. She imagined her baby son being sold by white slavers, run over by lorries and seduced by mad women. Dad laughed. 'Eleanor, for Christ's sake. He's having a wonderful time. He is twenty-one, precisely the right age to go to America, and at least he's sending postcards.' He looked at Mum's wretched face and took her hand. 'Come on. He's fine. You are too full of sensibility and somewhat lacking in sense.' Mum laughed and agreed not to worry, but continued to ask casual questions about mortality in the San Andreas fault.

Flook rang from San Francisco on Christmas Day. 'It's sunny, and I'm on my own,' he said, 'but it doesn't matter, because I can't imagine Christmas without being at home. This is just another day. I'll have Christmas next year.'

Brodie was hardly there either. Having worked for a year in the City he became dizzy with instant wealth, a commodity none of us was used to. After spending all the money on drink and drugs, he realized that banking was not for him. Uttering some crisply chosen phrases on the cynicism of exploitation, he traded his smart suits for a black-and-white guitar and a nose-ring. He formed a band by advertising for members in the *New Musical Express* and, soon after, they were sent to New York to record an album. Brodie came home on Christmas Eve, jet-lagged and unusually cheerful. His luggage was two bags of vanilla coffee and his guitar, his clothes were those he was wearing.

'I forgot everything else. I suppose I'll have to go back and get my stuff.' Mum and Dad were surprised at his good humour. He even said he liked his Christmas presents.

'Did you have a religious experience in New York?' Dad teased.

Brodie was so tired he missed the joke. 'No, I didn't see any churches. Actually, I never got further uptown than Greenwich Village.'

I was disgusted. 'You mean you didn't go to the Metropolitan Museum, or Tiffany's, or the Guggenheim?' I squawked.

Brodie sighed. 'I was working, you know. We never got out of the studio before two in the morning.'

Dad interrupted as I began to make a retrospective sight-seeing timetable for Brodie and the band. 'Va Va, you don't understand,' said Dad. 'Rock stars disappear in daylight. They require night and a little stimulation, isn't that so, Brodie?' Brodie grinned. He started discussing downtown bars with Dad who, despite not having visited New York for fifteen years, could remember almost all the ones Brodie mentioned. 'Brodie's smiled three times in half an hour,' said Poppy as we criss-crossed sprouts at the kitchen table. 'He must have had fun.'

Dan's girlfriend Tamsin came for Christmas lunch, bringing her own meat-free platter. Small, neat and blonde, she was a nurse he had met on his most recent stay in hospital. At ten o'clock in the evening, our lunch was ready. All day we had peered into the Aga, to be met with dough-coloured turkey. It sweated and hissed but would not cook. Finally Dan poured some paraffin into the Aga. It boomed from its heart and puffed into action, the hotplate turning angry red, then glittering pink with heat. Tamsin's nut roast cowered beside the vast turkey when Poppy and I heaved it out of the oven. It was wedged with forgotten logs we had put to dry in the Aga days before. The turkey had a strong woody taste which we all decided we might as well like. 'If we don't we won't eat for days,' said Dan, his plate a small mountain leaping with an avalanche of peas.

On the day after Boxing Day, Brodie and I left for London. I went with him to the airport, and he flew back to America for six more weeks. I returned to work, noisily tapping at my typewriter to draw attention to the fact that I was in the office between Christmas and New Year. No one was very interested.

Five orange kittens rolled across the kitchen floor. Patrick nudged one on to the toe of his boot. 'Catch!' he called to Flook, day-dreaming by the Aga.

'No, Daddy,' Va Va screamed, too late. The kitten was airborne, legs and tail spread wide like a star as it somersaulted towards Flook. Patrick laughed maniacally. Flook reached to catch it, but the kitten slipped through his fingers and landed on the Aga. It squealed, tinny and barbed with terror, then jumped down, scuttling sideways like a crab to hide under the dresser. The room smelt of singed fur, acrid and nauseating. Flook lay by the dresser, trawling his arms against the back wall, searching for the kitten. Va Va ran to Patrick, hitting him and screaming. Patrick was speechless. He tried to put his arms around her but she pushed him away. 'It's all right. My love, I am sorry, believe me.' His voice was cowed and pleading.

Her nose ran. 'I'll tell the RSPCA,' she screeched. Flook, cradling the now purring kitten, yelled too. Eleanor came in. Va Va opened her mouth to tell her what had happened but the words gagged. She could not say, 'Daddy hurt the kitten.' Patrick explained, halting and ashamed, like a child. Eleanor hugged Va Va and Flook. 'Darlings, the kitten is fine. Why don't you get him some milk? Daddy was very wrong to kick him, but it was entirely, entirely an accident that he hurt the kitten. Will you give him a kiss and let him say sorry?'

They calmed down, but the image stayed with Va Va. Every time she thought of it her stomach slipped sideways because Patrick had been cruel and she couldn't bear him not to be perfect. He never kicked the cats again.

On New Year's Eve, Mummy and Daddy went to a party. Helen had come to stay again, and she and Rex roared off on a motorbike, outriding Mummy and Daddy. Helen looked ill. She was very pregnant, and her face was swollen as well as her stomach. Mummy tried to stop her going on the motorbike, but she wouldn't listen.

'Heart of my heart, daughter of mine, you are a bloody idiot,' said Daddy, watching Helen scoop her hair into a yellow helmet. She rolled her eyes like an exasperated teenager and winked at me as she bundled out of the door in Rex's spare leathers. 'They never let you grow up, you know,' she whispered.

Zoe and Vinnie arrived in a taxi from Liza's house. They had brought presents for us all. Zoe and I bustled about lighting the fire and enjoying having the house as our own, without parents.

Before midnight, Helen and Rex were back, their leather clothes sparkling with frost. They were drunk. Brodie had taken down the oval mirror from above the fire and we stuck candles on to it with wax drops to celebrate the New Year. Dan and

Poppy were asleep in the playroom, their eyes shuttered against Benny Hill as he whooped and insinuated across the television screen. The rest of us grouped around the mirror, glasses filled with stolen wine, poised for midnight. Rex lurched head first on to the sofa, kicking one of the candles over.

'Watch out, this is a mirror,' said Brodie, alarmed by the large, creaking presence.

Rex leapt up, his face a snarl, long yellow teeth bared, pointed like peeled nuts. 'All a mirror does is bring you bad luck,' he jeered. Smiling unpleasantly, he picked the mirror up and threw it, shattering silvered splinters in the glowing fire. Then he turned on Brodie.

'Leave him alone,' screeched Helen, and I grabbed Rex's arm, pulling hopelessly at his sleeve. He whipped back his shoulder to shake me off and towered over Brodie, reaching to grab him out of the shadows. From the playroom, Big Ben tolled midnight as Zoe, Helen and I heaved and rocked with Rex. He shook me off again, hitting my nose with his elbow. My eyes watered, and I squeezed past him and knelt with Brodie. 'Go away. Leave us alone,' I sobbed. Rex whirled round, breaking two glasses and standing on Zoe's foot.

'You bastard.' Helen was at his throat, her face white fury, veins raised and pumping as she reached for his neck. Rex roared and punched her, then bounded over the sofa and out into the garden. Helen wiped her nose, smearing a trickle of blood across her cheek. She laughed shakily. 'Happy New Year, you lot,' she said.

After New Year, winter unfurled sharp claws and slashed deep into the earth, freezing the ground and drawing all colour and life out of trees and plants until everything was grey. Feeble snowflakes fell hesitantly from an ice-white sky, and ceased; it was too cold for the soft comfort of snow. From my bedroom I looked out at Shalimar, a soft black blur huddled beneath an oak tree.

Downstairs, Mummy was the only person who would talk to Bertrand Bougie, the French exchange student whom Brodie had visited in Paris last summer. Le Boogy, as the boys called him, was not a success. He sat at the kitchen table, his hair shiny and slicked down as if a tin of treacle had been poured over his head. As he sat he fiddled miserably with a cold piece of toast. At the beginning of his visit, Brodie and Flook had invited him to come and admire their collection of army gear. They gave him a gun to shoot rabbits with and offered their most prized unexploded shell for him to polish.

The shell, and other pieces of live ammunition, had been found when an American airforce plane hurtled into the field across the river. We came home from school one day to find khaki-clad soldiers guarding the white bridge at the edge of the village. Brodie and Flook were overjoyed. They were always delighted when a plane crashed nearby. Scrambling out of the car, they made friends with the soldiers, wheedling and cajoling until they were taken to the wreckage of the plane. There Flook absorbed the two young Americans in conversation, while Brodie, unnoticed, picked glinting explosives out of the twisted metal and mud and stuffed them under his blazer. They hid their booty in the hayloft, and only those armed with the password 'raphonidomai' (a word Mummy had taught us in our infant Greek lessons, meaning 'I stick a radish up the fundament') might enter. The boys were wary of Mummy discovering their treasured armoury, and although I was terrified and begged them at least to defuse their weapons, I knew I could not sneak.

But Le Boogy, an uncomprehending alien ill-clad for the Norfolk winter in neat shirts and sharply creased shorts, did not appreciate the honour of entering the hayloft. He sidled out, smiling and nodding, and went back to the warmth of the kitchen. He read comics and munched chocolate from a secret supply he stashed behind Mummy's French dictionary. He was afraid of animals and horrified by dirt. He clung to Mummy's kindness as if it were the last drop of human affection he would ever receive, and he went everywhere with her. Mummy urged me to be nice to him. 'Please, couldn't you talk to him? Tell him what you learnt in French or something. He's so lonely,' she begged in a desperate whisper, using a moment when Le Boogy was rootling for another bar of chocolate on the musty bookshelf. But I refused, retreating to the telephone for an hour-long string of inanities with Sasha. Brodie and Flook, exasperated at the failure of their overtures, and unable to offer Le Boogy anything more thrilling than ammunition, simply ignored him and went on with their ever more sophisticated and bloody war games.

So Le Boogy went to Mr Cardew's with Mummy, he went to the Norwich hairdresser with her, and he went shopping in Aylthorpe with her. This he enjoyed, bustling ahead of the supermarket trolley, his rounded rump swinging as he made for the cheese counter and the chocolate biscuits. Mummy allowed him to choose his favourite things, and his responsibility made him forget his homesickness a little. Le Boogy brought home piles of smoked cheese, tins of sardines, packets of garlic sausage and plastic tubs bursting with coiled salted herrings. We were all appalled. 'What's this gross stuff?' asked Brodie, holding up a thin, viscous anchovy. 'It looks like a worm. I'm not eating it. Why can't we have fish fingers?' Le Boogy looked at him astonished and went on tucking into his own plate of anchovies, pâté and olives.

Mummy still wore the blonde wig when driving. Daddy thought that driving lessons, like buying the cats and dogs tinned food instead of giving them scraps, were a waste of money, and flew into a spitting frenzy if he discovered Mummy was taking them. She somehow kept up a secret weekly tryst with her driving instructor. Although Mr Ball bowed to her insistence occasionally and let her take a driving test, each time fear paralysed her and she failed. Le Boogy became accustomed to the last-minute search for the wig, and solemnly hunted it out. He offered it to her, watching with unblinking concentration as she wedged it on to her head. She found his gaze unnerving, and once forgot to take off her beret before applying the wig. Le Boogy silently rose from the rocking-chair beside the Aga. Climbing up on to another chair next to Mummy, he gently removed the wig and then the beret. He replaced the wig with great care, tweaking it a little like a couturier addressing the final fitting of a gown. He spoke not a word as he completed the adjustments and climbed down.

He had never referred to the wig at all. Mummy had been

attempting unsuccessfully to construct an answer to the inevitable question and was relieved when Le Boogy's last day came and he had still not commented on her disguise. But preparing for the final shopping trip, Le Boogy, wig in hand, having retrieved it from the dog chair in the playroom, shook his head sorrowfully and looked up at Mummy with his great bovine eyes. 'Why you do this thing, Madame, why?' he pleaded, and Mummy was astonished to find herself answering firmly, 'It is a British custom.' Le Boogy smiled happily and nodded, a weight lifted from his mind, and they drove to Aylthorpe to purchase some offal, Le Boogy's special request for his last supper.

Patrick gave Eleanor a barrel full of crooning white doves and she hung it in a tree in the Wilderness. The doves swooped and hovered over the children as they played on fallen trees and dug holes among the naked twists of roots. When the doves were settled happily in their new home, Patrick and Eleanor and baby Dan flew to Wisconsin, leaving the three older children on the drive, clutching their cats, trying not to cry. They had to go, said Eleanor, making tea automatically as she did at every crisis, every triumph, and to pass the days and hours when nothing else was happening.

'Daddy and I have to go to America because Daddy has to earn some money so we can go on living here. Dan is a baby so he has to come with us, but we need you all to stay here and take care of the house and the animals and to keep it all safe for when we come home.'

Va Va saw an opportunity to reign supreme. 'I'll look after everything. I'm seven and a half, that's old enough. I can buy food from Mr Cardew's.'

'Yes. But to help you and to drive you to school, Tarquin and

Mary Lou are coming to stay here with you. And Louise is just up the road if you need her.'

Brodie flopped over Eleanor's knee, pinning her down. 'Why can't they look after the animals so we can all go with you?'

Eleanor looked sad. 'We haven't got enough money to buy all those aeroplane tickets.'

Tarquin and Mary Lou cowered in the kitchen behind curtains of long hippy hair. They brought with them their pale baby, Lupin, thin like a parsnip with a snail trail of snot on his upper lip.

Young Canadian intellectuals, soft and fresh out of university, Tarquin and Mary Lou prepared to embark upon a rural idyll at Mildney. Mary Lou cooked brown rice, boiling it for hours on the sullen Aga, droning away about where rice came from and what a fabulous famine food it was. It didn't make the rice any nicer. Mary Lou's large eyes wobbled with tears as she dished out the fabulous famine food. Brodie spat out a mouthful, rubbing his fist in it so it slimed over the table. 'Why don't you send it to the starving babies then?' Mary Lou pursed her lips and cleared it up. Brodie and Va Va glanced at one another, scorn in their eyes. Why hadn't she made him wipe the table, or at least told him off?

Eleanor had left pages of instructions on the dresser about feeding the animals, paying the milkman, washing clothes. When Mary Lou went upstairs to change Lupin's nappy, Va Va pushed a chair across to the dresser and wrote: THE CHILDREN LOVE ICECREAM AND STEAK AND KIDNEY PIE. THEY HATE BROWN RICE AND ALL HIPPY FOOD.

Tarquin looked like Jesus. He had long shiny hair and a

139

wispy beard, he wore white flared trousers and a white shirt. Every morning he strode out to the Wilderness and stood in front of the doves, arms outstretched, eyes closed, in a state of near-beatification. He said he was feeding them, but the doves never flew down, as they did with the children, to take the grain from his hands. After a few weeks they departed in a gleaming cloud to join the wood-pigeons at Mosseymere.

Mary Lou's hair was not as long or as lustrous as Tarquin's and she stuttered and blinked when she spoke to the children. 'Come on, honeys, brush your teeth for your Mom.'

Her orders and suggestions were met with scorn. 'Mummy doesn't mind if we don't brush our hair or our teeth. Anyway, she's not here.' Flook buried his head in a towel after his bath. His fringe was long and tangled, it swung into his eyes so he crashed into walls and fell over. Mary Lou wanted to cut it. 'My Mummy cuts my hair, not you.' He flailed and fought and Mary Lou almost gave up, but not entirely. Each morning she brushed Flook's hair, then scraped back his fringe and secured it with a kirby-grip. He looked like Shirley Temple, but it was better than allowing Mary Lou to cut his hair. Although he was only four, Flook started school while Patrick and Eleanor were away. Mary Lou begged the teachers to take him because she couldn't cope. Flook was delighted; he was big now, like Va Va and Brodie.

Eleanor sent frequent letters to each of the children, with presents in them. Balloons, as big as faces before they were blown up, had unreadable squashed writing on them. The children lined up in front of poor thin Tarquin, begging him to inflate them. It took him all day, but finally at tea-time Tarquin lay limp on the lawn as the children charged over him, their balloons as big as Space Hoppers, chanting, 'Madison Wisconsin, Madison Wisconsin,' delighted to be able to read the words stamped across the balloons' curves.

Patrick and Eleanor and Dan went to New Orleans one weekend, and the sweltering skies turned Dan's wisps of hair into corkscrew curls. They returned to England where Va Va, Brodie and Flook waited, misting tiny patches of the vast glass windows at Heathrow as they watched the plane land.

G rudgingly, the weather improved and winter slouched away before an invasion of buds dripping pale green from still trees. Snowdrops marched across the lawn and the animals started their usual irritating ritual of fornication and non-stop howling. Honey conceived her third litter of puppies by Hector, the rapist collie dog who belonged to the local farmer, and I received a letter from James Merry-Curl.

Dear Gabriella,

I wonder if you would like to come and watch my end of term match. Imogen is coming with a few other people, and it would be great fun to see you again. I am in the team, so I'll be able to see you after the game.

Love James (Merry-Curl)

I had never been sent a letter by a boy before. It caused hours of glee for my brothers, not least because Merry-Curl had enclosed a photograph of himself looking mean and moody in a cravat and blazer.

'Va Va's got a boyfriend!' yelled Brodie, waving the photograph above his head and passing it to Flook, who at once drew a caricature and stuck both likenesses up on the dresser. Pink with embarrassment and delight, I tried to ignore the boys and tell Mummy about Merry-Curl.

'I don't know why he's written to me. I didn't like him at that party because he said we were weird.'

'Well, we're not weird,' said Mummy, 'and I think it would be fun for you to go to the match if you want to. After all, there will be lots of other people to talk to if Merry-Curl is irritating.'

So I went, driven by Imogen's father, and cocooned in smug importance because I alone among the party had been invited by a boy. Imogen's brother was also playing in the match, and her father was wearing an old school tie in honour of the occasion.

'How long have you been going out with James?' Imogen probed as we swooped silently towards the school in the comfortable, expensive-smelling car.

'I'm not going out with James. I've only met him once and I can hardly remember what he looks like.'

I was not looking forward to seeing Merry-Curl again, but I hoped that there would be other, more glamorous boys there. Perhaps even one like Byron.

> I saw thee weep – the big bright tear
> Came o'er that eye of blue;
> And then methought it did appear
> A violet dropping dew:
> I saw thee smile – the sapphire's blaze

Beside thee ceased to shine;
It could not match the living rays
That fill'd that glance of thine.

I pretended that this poem was written for me, and spent the morning before the match looking in the mirror trying to be a weeping violet. Not a success. The school playing-field did nothing to feed my hopes of finding love. Anoraks abounded, grey nylon, black nylon with yellow stripes, fawn and navy blue, inert and hanging limp from puny shoulders. It had not occurred to me to discover what game was being played, and I noted gloomily that it was rugger. I was not interested in rugger. Despair filled my lungs and throat at the prospect of standing on the touchline all afternoon.

I saw Amelia Letson and, relieved to find a diversion from the pitch, I smiled and waved. She ran over, eyes sparkling. 'Gosh, it's so nice to see you,' she gushed. 'I'm with my cousin Tom. He broke his collar-bone at a point-to-point yesterday.' Standing back from Amelia's cluster of friends was a tall, dark-haired boy. He wore a sling on one arm and was staring at his feet. His face was pale. He was not wearing an anorak. He was almost Byronic.

'Does he ride racehorses?' I was impressed.

'Yes, he wants to be a jockey. We're going to the café in town, Tom doesn't like rugby,' and she scuttled off again.

The match continued. The players turned blue with cold and black with mud as they raced pointlessly up and down the pitch. I sulked, avoiding Merry-Curl's smiling glances in our direction. I wanted to be in the café with Amelia and

144

Tom, fascinating Tom with my blazing sapphire smile and impressing him with my knowledge of horses. It was not to be. Imogen's brother Edward was kicked in the groin and carried off the pitch, white-faced and whimpering. Imogen's father, stony with rage, muttered, 'Appalling bad sports, the lot of them,' and bundled his agonized son into the car. 'Come on, girls, we're going home,' he shouted. Imogen and I apprehensively edged into the front seat together so that her brother could recline in the back. We did not dare look over at him, afraid of what we might see. I knew from fighting with my own brothers that a blow to the groin was male torture, and my inability to imagine it made it embarrassing and sordid, a maimed initiation into manhood. Imogen's father dropped me at the bottom of our drive. I slammed the car door behind me, vowing never to attend a match of any description again. A point-to-point would be much more romantic.

April 1989

Flook and I hitch-hiked to Norfolk for Easter. He was working as a set-painter for a small theatre and didn't have enough money for the train fare, and I had sold my Ford Cortina to two Rastafarians for twenty-five pounds. I told them I was selling it because a lot of its undercarriage had fallen off going round Hammersmith roundabout and I had not dared stop to collect it. They didn't care. They jumped into the car, tied a pair of crocheted red, yellow and green baby bootees to the mirror and screeched off. I bought some Easter eggs with the money and went to meet Flook at Redbridge tube station.

Flook was there already, sitting cross-legged on the bonnet of a big black car, drumming his fingers on his knees. Behind him, Redbridge roundabout was a quagmire of muddy pools where construction work had ceased for the holiday. Flook's leather jacket with the reclining busty blonde he had painted on the back stood like a dwarf behind the car, held upright by its own stiff folds. A red baseball cap rested jauntily on the collar. Flook jumped down when he saw me. 'Va Va, we've got a lift home.' He gestured to the car. 'I bumped into Jim last night, and he's driving back to Norfolk.'

'Who's Jim?' I whispered as Flook piled my bags into the boot.

'Haven't you met him? He's an old friend of mine. He's been away, all over the world, for the last few years. It's great to see him again.'

We got into the car. A man with curling black hair sat behind the steering wheel. His face was long, his jaw square, and across one cheek a glaring scar burned deep into his flesh. He grinned. 'You look like a Lincoln,' he said. 'I know all your brothers, and you look just like them.' His accent was Irish, and he talked fast.

'Jim's from Belfast.' Flook was rummaging to find a tape in the glove compartment. He turned the machine on, and I could only say 'Thank you for the lift' before the car filled with frantic music for the rest of the journey.

We reached Mildney at tea-time. Brodie was there already; his band had played a gig in Cambridge the night before, and they had dropped him off at the station. He and Poppy were drinking tea in the kitchen. Dan and Dad, both leaning on walking-sticks, joined them. Mum crouched on all fours in front of the Aga, a knife in her hand, levering small black meteorites from the oven. 'My God,' said Flook as we entered, 'I think Mum's been trying to cook.'

'Shut up.' Mum's voice was muffled as she delved deeper into the oven. 'It's the Hot Cross Buns. They were meant for tea yesterday, but I forgot them.' Jim bent to catch a bun which was hurtling towards a sleeping cat. 'It's hot!' Mum shrieked, but Jim grasped the sooty ball and threw it out into the yard. 'I've got asbestos hands,' he grinned.

147

'Who is this man of iron?' Dad demanded, and Jim was introduced after embracing Dan and Brodie.

'It's been a while since I saw this bunch,' he said to Dad, 'but I've been thinking about them a lot. Flook gave me a book of yours, and I took a picture of it for you.'

Jim pulled a photograph from his inside pocket. We crowded round him to see. It was a beach. Long yellow sands stretched towards a still grey sea. A rifle, its butt buried, stood tall where the waves broke. Slung in the belt, facing us, was a book and from its clean dust-jacket Dad's portrait stared out.

'A Kalashnikov.' Brodie's voice shook with almost religious awe.

'And Dad's *Collected Poems*,' said Dan, amazed. 'What are they doing with that gun?'

'It's in Kurdistan,' said Jim. 'I was there with the rebels three weeks ago. I thought Patrick might like it, from all the stories you lot told me about him.'

Dad pulled the picture from beneath Dan's nose. 'Let me see. Why, it's charming. Jim, my dear boy, I see you have a sense of humour. I must frame this.' Dad rose, gripping his walking-stick. He pocketed the photograph. 'This is mine' – he curled his lips in a monstrous snarl – 'and if I catch you boys trying to steal it there will be hell to pay.'

Flook turned to Jim. 'Dad's really pleased. But can you explain what exactly you've been doing for the past two years?'

Sipping tea and refusing proffered cigarettes, Jim told us how he had taken food, blankets and money out to Kurdistan. Moved by the rebels' plight, he had stayed, his Foreign Legion training standing him in good stead during the fighting.

Poppy and I, listening from our perch on the Aga rail, looked at one another, astonished. 'He's like Robin Hood,' Poppy whispered. 'I've never heard anything like it.'

Dad came back into the kitchen. He paused in the doorway, struggling for breath. 'Jim, I should like to have a drink with you. Look under that hat on the shelf.'

Jim lifted the black fur dome and pulled out a bottle. Brodie whistled low. 'You *are* in favour,' he whispered. 'Dad never shares his champagne with anyone.'

Dad winked at Jim. 'My children are too barbaric for this ambrosia. Let us drink to Peace.'

Jim stayed a day or two, then left for his own cottage a few miles away. Often when I rang after that weekend, Dad was out driving with Jim, or sitting talking in the playroom with him. Jim delighted in surprising Dad with outings and plans. By summer the dogs had given up barking at his car, and Dad had started Jim on a plan to build a dam across the river.

B rodie and Flook were locked in the cloakroom. I banged on the door to be let in and found them shaving the sides of Brodie's head. The basin was grey with foam and hair and Brodie's scalp looked like a newly-plucked chicken, pink and bald with a furry strip bristling down the centre.

'My God,' I gasped, 'Mummy will kill you.'

'She won't notice if I wear a hat. D'you think it's good?'

I thought it was horrible. His face looked older, the bones protruding naked where once they had been softened by hair. The solid curve of his cranium was at once thuggish and heartbreakingly vulnerable. 'It's brilliant,' I said stoutly, 'but I don't think you'll get away with it at school.'

'Well, they like short back and sides, don't they?' He scraped the razor delicately behind one ear. The tiny, crispy rasp of steel against lathered skin made me shudder, and I left them, closing the door carefully so that Poppy and Dan didn't go in and see. I was cross. Brodie had never before done anything significant without telling me, and he hadn't even needed my help. I knew that he and Flook had discovered punk; I had helped cover one of Daddy's old jackets in safety pins and padlocks, but it had

150

seemed more like an extension of our childhood dressing-up than a new existence.

I lay on the playroom floor and picked up Poppy's Cindy doll. Her glassy blue eyes and froth of blonde hair reminded me of Imogen, and I dressed her from the little pile of clothes Poppy had left beside her. But clad, Cindy looked too bawdy to be Imogen. Her jutting plastic bosom strained at the sensible white shirt I had chosen for her, and her legs stretched on and on. Irritated, I undressed her again and covered her in a white sheet. Poppy might like to operate on her.

Brodie emerged from the cloakroom, insouciant in a red and white woolly hat; I forbore to draw attention to it. 'Will you come and see Spear of Destiny tonight?' he asked, binding red strips of fabric torn from Mummy's old nightie around the sleeve of his dark-green cavalry officer's jacket. Spear of Destiny was Brodie's favourite band. They took their name and many of their lyrics from the Red Indian mythology which was his obsession, and he had a collection of their records and press cuttings stacked in his bedroom. I was very pleased to be asked, relieved not to be entirely excluded from Brodie's life.

Flook wanted to come too, but Mummy wouldn't let him. 'You're not old enough. You're only thirteen; no one will believe you are eighteen, and then all three of you will be barred.'

Flook was livid. 'Brodie only knows about Spear of Destiny because I gave him their record for his birthday.' He scowled, arms folded, rigid with dignity and the desire to be included. Daddy came in. Flook turned away, eyes warped with tears.

'My love, you have years of this sort of thing ahead of you. Va Va and Brodie never went when they were thirteen. It is dangerous.'

Dan shouted from the playroom, 'Come and help me fix my rollerskates.'

Flook trembled; snakelike and treacherous, Brodie and I left. Half-way down the drive, Brodie removed the woolly hat and replaced it with an old top hat decorated with bird skulls and rabbit bones. He had taken to boiling up the remains of creatures killed by the cats until the bones bobbed clean white in the saucepan. He laid them out to dry on the back of the Aga before sewing them on to his clothes. Mummy thought it was grotesque.

'I think he's got psychopathic tendencies,' she whispered to me. 'What shall I do?'

Daddy dismissed her worry with a wave of his hand. 'He is adorning himself like an Indian brave. It's marvellous, Eleanor. Don't bitch him up.'

Mummy sighed and swept a tiny foreleg into the rubbish. 'I suppose he'll grow out of it,' she said.

Merry-Curl had telephoned asking me to go out for a drink with him, so I persuaded him that he too would like to see Spear of Destiny, and he was to pick us up from the bottom of the drive. 'Why didn't you ask him to come to the house?' asked Brodie, as we waited in the mild spring dusk.

'I don't know. I was embarrassed, I suppose.'

'By him or by us?'

I reddened and did not answer. I was worried that Merry-Curl would be wearing the blazer and cravat he had favoured in his photograph, but he was sporting a perfectly acceptable leather jacket. Brodie became quite enthusiastic.

'Will you swap your jacket for a Royal Fusiliers one?' he asked hopefully, leaning forward between the two front seats.

Merry-Curl was a lot better than I remembered, and although my heart now belonged to the world of steeplechasers, I was prepared to be friends with him. He seemed more relaxed and older than he had at Imogen's party.

'I'm sorry you had to leave the match,' he said, 'It was a good game.'

'Yes, it looked great.' I turned round with narrowed eyes to scowl at Brodie sniggering in the back. 'Actually, I don't really understand rugby,' I admitted, desperate because Brodie's laughter was audible even though I had pinched him, and Merry-Curl was looking hurt.

We arrived at West Runton, a straggling seaside town where the golf course dropped straight over the cliffs and into the sea. In the heart of the town the façade of a gabled house loomed over bungalows, elaborate pediments throwing wild shadows across the boarded-up windows. Sprayed graffiti sprawled drunkenly, bawling barbarous messages at passers-by. 'Fuck the Queen' and 'God is doing time' blazed in our headlights as Merry-Curl parked the car. Behind the Queen Anne ruin a concrete building squatted; the dance-hall in which bands played to heaving audiences of punks and skinheads every weekend.

We walked to the ticket office past two green-haired boys wearing studded dog collars who sat hunched, breathing into crumpled plastic bags. I jumped as one keeled over in our path. He lay, back arched like an acrobat, eyes half closed, skin sticky with a sheen of sweat. Inside, the stage loomed dark across a floor empty except for a few plastic glasses. Shadowy movements in the gloom and the flare of matches illuminating pale, black-eyed faces were the only suggestions of an audience. The band plunged on to the stage. The floor swarmed. Forward they came, jostling leather-clad punks, hair in fiery crests or soaped in slimy spikes which trickled a sluggish wake down their backs. Faces smeared with kohl and pierced with safety-pins, lips wet and red, were turned up to the singer as he screamed his first song, almost swallowing the microphone.

From the other side of the room a roaring mass of bald, pasty figures stomped towards the stage. Their denim uniform flapped filthy, wounds in the fabric sewn together with raw red stitching and scarred by lumpy plastic tubes. The two waves surged towards the three of us, still and small by the stage. Brodie climbed on to a chair, unperturbed by the thrashing flesh around him. Merry-Curl left us to get a drink, and I relaxed a little and watched the band, enjoying the sensation of loud music vibrating through me. Someone pushed me, then someone else. I looked round and was terrified. I was some distance away from Brodie, and the punks were falling back in a swooping line like a drawn curtain. Brodie was beached on his chair and a steady cord of skinheads advanced towards him, led by a stout, short man. The man's brow gleamed where it was studded with metal squares; he scuttled forward, bent low like Quasimodo, mouth open in a silent roar, arms spread wide, waving half a smashed bottle in wild arcs. The band stopped playing, and the singer yelled into his microphone. 'Stop.

What the hell is going on here?' No one took any notice. Dropping their instruments, the band tiptoed off the stage. The skinhead line fragmented and roared towards the punks. Brodie remained isolated and still on his chair, white-faced, arms stiff at his side, a martyr preparing to be burnt at the stake. I expected every second that he would fall, drown in the heaving human sea, but he didn't. Somehow I was at the edge of the crowd, which slowed for a moment as people thrust their way through the door and burst out into the street. I ran back to Brodie through the empty hall. All the skinheads had gone. We were alone in the vast room, listening to muted shouts and screams and the approaching wail of police cars.

'Do you think the band will come on again?' Brodie smiled lopsidedly.

Merry-Curl came back. 'What's happened? Why has everyone gone?' He balanced our drinks on the edge of the stage. 'What have I missed?'

'I think we'd better go.' I was suddenly heavy with exhaustion and relief.

At home, Daddy and Flook were painting a fort for Dan. Flook, sleeves rolled back to his elbows, his face daubed with green and silver paint, had forgotten his anger. Daddy shook his head and looked intently at us as Brodie and I, with occasional interruptions from Merry-Curl, told of our adventure. The last wisps of fear evaporated like morning mist as we sat in the playroom drinking tea. Daddy dipped a warring knight in his tin of gold paint. 'Well, my loves, you were lucky, very lucky. But tell me, did you enjoy the music?'

Brodie's face lit up and he leaned forward over the table,

poised to list its many virtues. Merry-Curl and I retreated to the kitchen where Mummy sat reading. The last of Honey's puppies, a handsome buck whom we had named T-Shirt Smith because his white front legs protruded from his soft black torso like arms from a T-shirt, became vivacious in the presence of Merry-Curl. 'I'd love a dog,' said Merry-Curl, stroking T-Shirt into frenzies of delight by tickling his ears. Emboldened by his evening's experiences, Merry-Curl was expansive. 'My parents would go mad if I told them about the fight,' he said to me. 'Your family is really cool.'

Even Imogen admired Daddy. She came to stay one weekend and Daddy gave her a book about medieval courtship. 'Tell me, my dear, do you dream of salvation in shining armour?' he asked her, and I sighed, exasperated by his capacity for nonsense.

Imogen was captivated. 'Do all poets talk like your father? Will he write a poem about me?'

'Don't be ridiculous,' I snapped and dragged her up to my room to try on dresses for a party.

Patrick rushed in from the back yard banging the doors, pushing through with an armful of wood for the fire.

'There is nothing, nothing, between here and the North Pole.' His breath puffed white clouds in the cold air and he escaped into his warm study to work. Eleanor stayed, feeding the children, feeding the hens, feeding the dogs and cats and never seeing a soul. There was no money to pay a babysitter, so she could never leave the house alone unless she put Va Va, Brodie and Flook under Patrick's vague surveillance.

The day she went to Norwich to the hairdresser they found a tin of purple paint. Patrick lay in the yard beneath the Mercedes, the bulk of three coats wedging him secure from the whistling wind. Brodie hit the paint-pot lid with a hammer and a jet of foaming violet spurted in his face. Laughing, he smeared dirty hands across his eyes, spreading purple into his hair. 'Let's paint the pump,' suggested Va Va, and they set to work. The wind shrieked, but they were silent at their toil. Patrick, suspicious too late, came out from under the car to see where the children were. Flook was investigating the last of the paint and upended the tin over his boots.

'This is a goddam mess,' Patrick yelled. 'Your Mummy is going to be very cross unless we can clear the whole lot up.' He swept Flook into the house, a bright trickle of paint following them, and stood him in the kitchen sink. Va Va and Brodie scrubbed the pump, mauve water flowing at their feet. Wet through, they shivered, brushes clutched in numb hands, waiting for Patrick to tell them they had done enough.

He came out, followed by Flook wrapped in a towel. 'Now this is good work,' he puffed on his cigarette, 'but Mummy will see the paint.' Three pairs of anxious eyes implored. He laughed. 'We'll have to paint black over it so it looks like it did before.'

The pump looked smart with a new coat of black paint. Eleanor returned, Va Va saw her coming up the drive and shouted a warning to Patrick.

'Quick, quick,' he yelled, mock horror in his voice, 'into your places.'

The children shuffled on to their chairs, shifting plates on the table so that each of them had bread and butter and a cup of milk in front of them when Eleanor came in.

M uch changed that year, especially Brodie's and Flook's hairstyles. Each week brought a new patch of bald scalp to gleam beneath peaks of rainbowed hair. Mummy walked into the bathroom during a bleaching session. Flook, bare to the waist, sat on a chair in front of the mirror, his hair half white and half invisible, tucked away in neat silver foil pouches. Poppy and Dan perched on the edge of the bath, holding strips of foil and watching, absorbed, as Brodie worked.

'Jesus Christ! What are you doing to him?' Mummy screamed. Brodie jumped, spilling peroxide in a glut across Flook's naked shoulders. Flook leapt up roaring. Dan and Poppy flung down their foil and slunk out guiltily.

'This stuff is agony. Get it off me, get it off me!' Flook plunged his torso into the bath.

Behind him, Mummy rocked back and forth in rage, eyes narrowed, her lips tight and puckered white. 'How can you be so stupid? Thank God it's the summer holidays. Do you realize that in term-time you would be expelled for this, quite apart from the unutterable damage you are doing to your hair. And it looks ghastly.' She stalked out, slamming the door so hard that one of the panels fell out.

'I don't see what she's making such a fuss about.' Brodie continued to unwrap the foil parcels. Flook sat still, tensed like an old lady at the hairdresser's. 'We've been dyeing our hair for months.'

'I don't think she's ever really taken it in before,' replied Flook.

The boys told me about this row the next day. I had been out. Suddenly I was out a lot. Imogen's inexhaustible social energy and her desire to have someone to giggle with made her invite me to the many parties she was asked to that summer. I stayed with her for a weekend which grew into a week, enjoying the world away from my family and absorbing luxury with heady greed.

Everything at Imogen's house operated like clockwork. Her mother drifted into the walled garden carrying a trug, and beheaded limp roses while Imogen and I lay by the stinging blue pool, inhaling the scent of honeysuckle mingled with chlorine. Delicious lunches of cold salmon and crisp salad appeared like magic at one o'clock, and no one ever came and told us to feed the hens or muck out the stables. Imogen's brother Edward was given a little blue car and he taught me to drive it, trundling through a hayfield, weaving erratically between vast cotton-reel bales.

At night I lay in a sprigged bower, stretching my limbs over stiff linen sheets and looking up at the ruby canopy of a four-poster bed. I wallowed in soft comfort and thought of my room at home: the slanted ceiling dotted with Blu-Tack where my horse pictures had fallen down; the bed, its chipped paint surrounding a gaping hole in the wickerwork, excavated, I was sure, by busy mice as I slept. I thought of the cobwebs rattling with the last throes of flies, of the bathroom where the taps in the basin had not worked since I was four, and of the fridge full of nothing more sustaining than a pool of milk spilt from an overturned bottle. I tried to think of something my home had in common with Imogen's; some small corner of it which mirrored the smooth, structured existence at Wallby Hall. There, flowers swanned on graceful stems above gleaming polished tables, and a lady in a blue nylon coat, a yellow duster in her pocket, vaccumed and scrubbed every morning. At home there were dog hairs on the carpet and springs rearing like serpents from the sofas. Mummy picked bunches of wild flowers, thrusting cow parsley and hogweed into buckets and urns and placing them, towering and sweet-scented, on a mantelpiece where they stayed until they had become ghosts, skeletal and colourless, with the scent of old hay. No one cleaned our house. Mummy once had a vacuum cleaner, a green globe which coasted proudly along the landing for a week after Trixie had donated it. But Mummy failed to love it, and one day negligence toppled it down the stairs and on to the flagstones in the hall with a splintering crunch, followed by a high-pitched moan. After that it would only exhale air, and soon became a home for Martians in the playroom.

The only element of Imogen's house which faintly echoed Mildney was the library. Imogen's grandfather had collected books, and his passion was ranked neatly from floor to ceiling in a high panelled room. Imogen never went in there, dismissing the books as 'really ancient and dull', but I loved it. It reminded me of home, where every corridor and room was panelled with books piled one upon another.

At lunch, talking to Imogen's father about his books as his moustache bounced above his masticating jaws, I oozed superiority when he said, 'Of course, the library is very fine, but nothing to the one your father must have.'

'Well, we haven't got a room full of books like your one,' I answered cautiously, longing but not daring to lie, 'but there are a lot there, and I think Daddy has read every one of them, and Mummy too.'

'Extraordinary,' said Imogen's father, and the moustache sat inert for a second while he wiped it with his napkin, like a good dog waiting for praise. 'I only read the *Shooting Times* myself, but they always say "horses for courses", don't they?' The moustache shot off again in pursuit of a spoonful of summer pudding.

Filing into the Drinking Room to give Patrick a good-night kiss on a Saturday, the children lined up in front of him.

'My angel, thou art precious,' he said. Va Va squirmed. Ben and Joe, the boys' best friends, were staying and she was sure that their father didn't talk like Patrick.

'Talk properly, Daddy,' Brodie whispered, and Patrick let his shoulders droop.

'Dear God. Is there no freedom from policing in a man's own home?' He smiled an annoying soppy smile and stroked Brodie's hair. 'Brave child. Thou wilt break my heart.' Brodie and Va Va sighed. It was useless. Patrick winked at Ben. 'Tell me, young man, exactly how old are you now?'

'Seven,' said Ben.

'Seven. It is my belief that all children should remain seven for ever and ever.'

'What about me, Daddy?' Va Va interrupted, anxious. 'I'm eight.'

Patrick hugged her. 'You, heart of my heart, are a sophisticate, and sophisticates cannot be controlled.' Va Va was pleased by this. She savoured the word, whispering it as she went up to

163

bed. It was a good word, it sounded like lace and scent and cigarettes. It sounded so feminine that Va Va fancied the word wore lipstick and had long curling red hair.

Patrick looked at Eleanor as she ushered the children out. 'Dear heart, do not allow these bambini in here when I am in my cups.'

Imogen and I were to go to a party that evening. Sitting in her room preparing ourselves, we discussed who might be there. I still nurtured a secret desire to meet and spellbind Tom the racehorse rider. I had seen him several times, but had never dared speak to him, terrified that my infatuation might be visible and mocked.

'Amelia will be there, won't she?' I strained with the effort to sound casual. 'She seems to spend a lot of time with her cousin Tom, doesn't she?'

Imogen was painting her tiny mouth pale pink with a delicate brush and a pot of gluey lip gloss. 'She's very keen on him,' she mumbled. 'And she knows it makes her more popular to be with him, because all the girls have crushes on Tom.' Absorbed, she didn't see the prickly flush spread across my face. We went downstairs to find Edward, who was driving us.

The party was in a small flint barn sunk deep into a fold of curving pasture, two miles from the nearest road. A paint-spattered sheet draped over the door was the only attempt at decoration; the rest of the barn was bare. A friend of Edward's sat on the floor, a screwdriver and a tape recorder in his hands. 'The music has packed up,' he said gloomily as we entered.

Imogen and I stood by the door and looked across the hazy summer fields. An occasional car lumbered towards us, depositing brightly clad partygoers who tripped giggling into the barn, and then stood like a disconsolate herd of cows in the corner by the barrel of beer. Intermittent squawks and groans issued from the tape machine; the only other sounds were nocturnal twitterings from sleepy birds and the neurotic, ceaseless whisper of wind in the trees. Tom and Amelia arrived in a tiny, grunting mini-moke. This confirmed my high opinion of Tom. Very few others found the barn. At midnight, bored and sober, Edward decided to leave. Tom and Amelia followed us. We skidded over shorn hayfields back on to the road. I sat in the front with Edward, my feet up on the glove compartment of the car, and leaned back looking out of the sun-roof at pale stars in the deep purple sky.

'Tom is really messing around,' said Edward, as the mini-moke zoomed past us on a bend. I sat up as we rounded the corner. There, squat and stationary, music blaring and lights flashing, was the mini-moke.

'We're going to crash,' said Edward, trying to swerve, but we were going too fast and I watched with curious detachment as we smashed into the mini-moke. My head hit the windscreen and cold glass splintered in my hair and on my face. My shins were thrust into the dashboard as the car spiralled into the roadside.

'Get out! For Christ's sake get out!' yelled Edward. 'There's another car coming.' Imogen scrambled out from the back and I tried to open my door. It was buckled and stuck. I did not dare to move, or even look round. Blood oozed warm on my face; if I moved, I knew the slow sticky bleeding would burst into a torrent. Motionless in heaped dead metal, I watched through the hole my head had made in the windscreen as the others ran and stopped in shocked, uncertain circles.

Edward and Tom pushed the cars off the road and pressed themselves back on the bank. A sweep of headlights came towards us. Imogen was still trying to let me out. 'Are you all right? Oh, God, she's got blood on her face. Edward, come here quick!' Edward came just as the door yielded. He sank back on the verge. 'Oh God, what have I done?' he whispered. And finally I cried, terror at his expression pumping tears until I heaved with breathless, hysterical sobs.

Daddy came to collect me from Imogen's house the next morning. He looked very angry until we got into the car. Then he said, 'Darling heart, thank God you're not hurt. That tiny cut on your face will be gone in a week.' I wept, and he took my hand. 'Look at me.' I did. He was smiling. 'My love, it will not spoil your beauty, so don't cry.'

Two weeks later my face was healed, and after a series of lengthy, tiring telephone calls and visits, I finally persuaded Edward that it was not his fault. Secretly I enjoyed my role as most damaged victim of a car crash. I stayed at home, craving comfort and receiving it in cups of hot chocolate and rolls of loo paper to cry into. Mummy was furious, feeding my sense of martyrdom by shouting in bouts lasting a few minutes every day. 'How can you be so idiotic as to let yourself be driven by drunken louts?'

I said nothing, bowing my head, bearing my undeserved haranguing. Maimed and misjudged, I thought to myself.

Daddy intervened. 'Eleanor, I think she's learnt her lesson. Let's hear no more of it.' Mummy fumed and humphed for a while longer, but eventually gave up, distracted by Poppy, who, aged eight, had decided to become a vegetarian.

V a Va woke early and looked up at the ceiling, focusing her eyes to make faces emerge from the wavering pattern of cracks. She raised her arms, fingers reaching out, twisting in the little puffs of smoke which sailed above her bed. The smoke thickened dull grey, and she got out of bed to turn the light on. 'It looks like a lighthouse,' she thought, climbing back into the warm hollow and lying flat, concentrating until the ceiling cracks metamorphosed into boats and waves on the ocean.

Brodie sat up, coughing. 'There's a fire. Quick, we must tell Mummy.' He scuttled out of the nursery holding his sagging pyjamas up with one hand. Va Va followed, speechless at her own stupidity and her missed opportunity to be the heroine of the hour.

Patrick came running down the landing, a jersey tied like an apron around his waist. The study door was shut and from beneath it woolly strands of smoke unravelled.

'Open the door!' yelled Patrick, and Va Va remembered that a man with a crinkled yellowing beard had come to stay. He had said he was her godfather. 'Let us in, Kevin. Let us in!' Va Va was anxious to see the fire before it was put out.

169

When Kevin opened the door, his face was black and he had a blanket wrapped around him. A cheery blaze crackled in the waste-paper basket.

'You fool, you're supposed to put the blanket over the fire.' Patrick tugged a flapping corner of Kevin's shroud and sent him spinning across the room. Wielding the huge folds of blanket, Patrick threw himself on to the burning basket, groping and wrestling until he had a clumsy parcel. He stood up, bellowing, 'Watch out, children!' and charged out of the room and down the stairs. Va Va and Brodie ran after him, but he was already outside, his naked limbs catching the sunlight on the river where he splashed, trying to drown the flames.

It was nearly the end of the summer holidays, and I had to make a skirt for the sixth form. I sat, as I had done every day since the accident, composed but forlorn on the sofa in the playroom, cushioned by Honey's plump sleeping form. Louise tacked my skirt together for me, and I began to hem it, struggling with unyielding tweed. Staring mindlessly at the television I moved my tongue around the inside of my mouth, feeling for the hundredth time the rough bump of the inside of my cut. Music blared out as the local news programme began.

'The headlines tonight. Dereham protests against bypass plans. Norfolk beaches are under threat from litter-lout tourists, and Tom Letson, elder son of Robin Letson the racehorse trainer, has been killed. The tragedy occurred when his horse fell while he was competing at the Byborough County Show this afternoon. The horse, Dancing Rainbow, was also injured, and had to be shot.'

Excitement at hearing Tom's name on television turned to cold horror as the reporter completed his announcement. Dead. Killed. Tragedy. Shot. The words swarmed in my head. I stood up, limbs heavy and stomach contracted, and turned off the television before stumbling through to the kitchen. I tried to tell Mummy, but no words would come out. Instead I was sick, coughing and sweating over the sink. Mummy bathed my face with an old floorcloth which smelt of cat pee. I spluttered, she led me to a chair.

'Darling, what is it? Are you hurt? What has happened?' She leaned over me, stroking my hair. 'It's delayed shock from your accident. I must ring the doctor. Sit there and sip this water.'

I grabbed her arm and shook my head, another wave of nausea rising. 'No, not me. I'm fine. It's Tom, Amelia's cousin. He's been killed. I saw it on television. I can't believe it. It's not fair.'

I bent forward and rocked in the chair, trying to focus the thoughts swarming in my head. Mummy wrapped her arms around me, murmuring.

Daddy appeared. 'What's the matter in here?' Mummy told him. He went out, and came in a moment later with a glass half full of brown liquid. It smelt bitter and pungent. 'Drink this, love, it will steady you.'

His gentleness calmed me. I drank the brandy, shuddering again at the hot taste. It stopped the whirling thoughts and filled the emptiness of shock. I wiped my eyes, and Daddy gave me a cigarette. 'I know you are not supposed to smoke these things,' he said, raising one eyebrow, 'but needs must when the Devil rides.' I began to feel safe again. 'Now tell me what has happened to this young man.' Daddy took my hand and sat down next to me.

'I saw it on television – he's been killed at a horse show. I didn't know him well, but he was the one we crashed into the other day. He was very handsome.' I began to cry. Big splashy tears chased down my nose and dribbled on to my hand and into my glass.

Daddy took his red handkerchief and dried my eyes. 'I must tell you something serious; it offers no comfort, but is beautiful. "Whom the gods love die young." Your friend was a special young man, and he will remain that for ever. You will not forget him, nor will he ever become less than he is to you now. And he will never change. Do you understand me?' Daddy's voice splintered harsh in the silent kitchen. Mummy gave me another cigarette, and brought in the bottle of brandy.

When I was twenty-four, Mum told me she and Dad were getting married. 'So that's why there aren't any wedding photos,' was all I could think of to say. And she explained how Dad had never been able to divorce Nancy, his first wife, whom he hadn't seen for thirty years. Now poor Nancy had died, shrivelled into senile dementia by her bitter angry life. She had resented him too much to free him. I was shocked, and surprised at my shock. When the boys and Poppy were told, Mummy laughed till tears ran down her face, apologizing as she choked, because each one of them said, 'So that's why there aren't any wedding photos.' Mum wrote a list of friends and family to invite to the wedding and I looked on in silence. Dad came in and kissed the top of my head. 'Scandalous, isn't it?' he mocked, and I suddenly felt moved and thrilled. To be at one's parents' wedding was a rare privilege, I decided.

The weeks before the wedding were fraught. While banns were read each week at the Catholic church in Sallingham, we made late-night phone calls to California, trying to track down Nancy's death certificate. It arrived at last, and we celebrated with a bottle of red Martini. For once, Dad shared.

The garden was blooming; tangles of roses struggled across walls, petals like drops of blood where tendrils had paused on the grey flint. Dad wore a white suit, his bootlace tie secured with a silver eagle stolen from Brodie. His feet were large and pneumatic in a pair of pumped-up Reeboks which belonged to Dan. Dad was very pleased with them and spun a football on the lawn. The boys watched gravely, terrified that he might hurt himself but unable to dent his pride by stopping him. Mum wore black, her dress sprigged with white flowers and comfortingly familiar. It was the one she wore for all godly events, from carol services to funerals, and she would consider no alternative.

At the church, Action Priest waited, preening in his ceremonial robes. Flook named him Action Priest when he saw the boyish figure, head close-cropped, features lean and muscular, getting out of a sports car one day at Mildney. He had come to hear Dad's confession. While Mum and I skulked nervously in the house, Action Priest went out to the lawn where Dad was sitting. 'He hasn't been to confession once since I've known him,' Mum whispered. 'I hope he's not going to say something disgraceful.'

One and a half minutes later Dad appeared, leaning heavily on Action Priest's arm; they walked towards the arbour for an absolving drink. Smiling and joking, they passed us peering out of the back door. Dad pretended not to see us, but he looked back and winked, curling his lips back to utter a triumphant 'Hah' at his lurking, incredulous family. We allowed a decorous interlude to pass, then crept round to the arbour. They were talking about football, Dad's arm around Action Priest as they moved goal by goal through the League table.

*　　　*　　　*

Squat and new, the church hung over Sallingham's white cliffs, high above wheeling gulls and a glittering black sea. Dad refused to sit on the chair placed for him in front of the altar. We heard his breath coming heavy and slow as he performed his role. Mum shook as she made her vows, her voice trembling, almost swallowed by the rustle and creak of the congregation. Afterwards we threw confetti over them and Dan pulled up in his rusting white Vauxhall car. It was wet with sequins and hearts hastily daubed that morning over Dan's Bob Marley emblem. He drove Mum and Dad away, leaving the scent of smouldering rubber on the road behind him.

Back home in the garden, guests queued up to salute Mum and Dad while Brodie, Flook, Dan, Poppy and I stood behind, smiling proudly, as if we were the parents.

The next day, Dad and Poppy flew to Italy for the honeymoon. Mum went on the train. 'I want to enjoy our honeymoon,' she insisted, 'and I won't if aeroplanes are involved.'

It was August. Italy sweated and scorched under a blistering sun. Dad became ill, his throat parched and closed against the hot air. Late one night he was rushed to hospital in Siena. He stayed there for a month.

Poppy returned to England, white and thin. I met her at the airport and she fell crying into my arms. 'It was terrible. I found Dad collapsed in the bathroom,' she gulped. 'I thought he was dead, his skin was cold. He had to go to hospital on the third day we were there, and since then all we've done is drive to Siena to sit in his little hot room with him. Mum won't come

176

back until he's let out, and the doctors don't know how to make him better.'

I was terrified that Dad would die. On his honeymoon, in Italy, the place he loved, with Mum, the person he loved. Hysteria rising, I knew that this was how the gods had destined it to be. A day later, Mum rang from a hospital phone. 'You might have to come,' was all she said when I asked how he was. 'Let's give it another day.'

Poppy and I lashed ourselves into fevered misery, then Flook phoned and told us not to be so bloody stupid. 'He's only ill because it's hot.' He spoke slowly, enunciating very clearly, as if talking to an imbecile. 'He'll be fine when he gets home.'

Thoughts of his never getting home faded with Flook's words. Two days later, a long white car drew up at Mildney. Out came Mum, pale and blotched, with dark-ringed eyes. Out came Dad, wrapped in a white cashmere blanket, suntanned and wearing dark glasses. He was thin. Bones I had never noticed before were crossed by veins fragile as birds' feet, and his nose reared patrician in his sunken face. We prepared to carry him, reverential and praising the Lord, into the house, but he would have none of it. Seizing his stick, he walked round to the front of the car and asked the driver to raise the bonnet. Poppy and I gawped. Dad and the driver began to examine the engine.

'He's thrilled by this car,' whispered Mum. 'As soon as he saw it, he cheered up. He's been talking about engines all the way from the airport.' We made Mum some tea. Dad did not appear for half an hour.

O n my seventeenth birthday I took my first driving lesson and tasted independence. A-levels were looming, but their significance receded in the face of three-point turns and hill starts. I was relieved to find that I had inherited driving skills from Daddy rather than Mummy, and took my test three months later.

In the car park outside the test centre, my examiner, who smelt strongly of cheese biscuits, licked his lips until they shone wet pink and said, 'Miss Lincoln, I am happy to tell you that you have passed your test. Congratulations.' I remembered stories of people embracing their examiners at this moment, but although elation pounded in my heart, I had no urge to get any closer to Mr Tibbins. I ran across the car park to Mummy; she was reading the Highway Code. She fumbled with the car door when she saw my face.

'I've passed! I've passed! I can't believe it, Mummy, I've passed.' We embraced, staggering back and forth in front of our car.

'Do you think it's a good omen for me, or a bad one?' asked Mummy when we were in the car and I was driving proudly towards school. Mummy was taking her test a week later, and had ordered tranquillizers from the doctor.

'I bet you'll pass too. It must be a good omen.' I executed a substandard manoeuvre and parked clumsily outside school.

'I can always pretend I'm you if I fail,' Mummy shouted, as I ran in through the school gates feeling lithe, successful and confident.

Deflation in the form of an unseen Latin translation awaited me. I was the only pupil taking A-level Latin, so there was no one I could hide behind. Honesty was the best policy.

'I'm awfully sorry, Miss Doball.' I ran my fingers through my hair and schooled my face into an expression of appealing contrition. 'I haven't learnt any Latin this week because I've been doing the Highway Code. I've just passed my driving test, you see.'

Miss Doball, her face white and bunched like a crumpled paper bag, shied back on her chair and shrieked at me. 'What use is a driving test to a Latin scholar! You are not applying yourself. You don't know even the most basic grammar. I am beginning to doubt your ability, Gabriella, I really am. We shall attempt Virgil now. Do not fail me, I beg of you.'

Furious at Miss Doball's reaction I opened Virgil. The words became gibberish before my eyes, and I fidgeted with frustration. I had not even read through the text. Desperate but still spiked with bravado, I closed the book. 'I don't know this, but I've learnt some Catullus. Shall I recite it?'

Miss Doball's ivory knuckles twitched; she pushed her glasses further up her sharp nose and sighed, rasping and brief. 'If you must, but it's not on the syllabus; however, I'm delighted to hear that you are reading round the subject.'

I began, standing up to recite, hands clasped behind my back, eyes modestly lowered:

> 'Thallus you pansy, softer than rabbit's wool,
> The down of a goose or the lobe of an ear,
> Softer than an old man's penis and the cobwebs
>   hanging from it.
> Thallus none the less rapacious . . .'

'*That will do*,' stormed Miss Doball. 'You are insolent and unteachable.' Taking off her glasses, she picked up her books and scurried out of the classroom, anger stamped in red spots on her knobbly cheeks. I remained at my desk, smirking defiance at the blackboard, trying to ignore shame as it scratched and burnt its way up my body. 'She should know what Catullus is like,' I muttered sulkily; to assuage my guilt I spent the next hour learning Virgil off by heart.

At lunch-time, a small girl with freckles and a brace found me. 'The headmistress wants to see you in her study,' she piped, then whisked away with her giggling companions. Sweat rose on my palms and breathing became shallow and painful as I knocked on the headmistress's office door.

Miss Floyd was looking out of the window. In her long black gown, with her mouth turned down and her expression cold and unamused, she looked like an executioner. I had a hysterical urge to laugh and bit my tongue.

'Miss Doball tells me that you had a disagreement this morning.' She swivelled her head towards me, lashless eyes unblinking as a baldheaded eagle viewing its prey. 'Mrs Benton tells me that you have not written a single history essay this term. Mr Graymer tells me that you have written no essays for your A-level class, and have insisted that your English scholarship class is enough work.' She turned her bulk at last; I stood with one leg twisted around the other, as near the door as possible. 'What have you to say for yourself, Gabriella?'

Rage erupted and rushed headlong through me. With both feet braced against the floor, my fists clenched, my eyes bulging with a vision of freedom, I said, 'It is typical of the staff here to tell tales without consulting the person concerned. I have nothing to say except that I have no respect for my teachers, and although I want to do my A-levels, I won't work for those teachers. I should like to leave this school and do the rest of my A-level work at home.'

Immediately my anger evaporated. I slumped, almost over-balancing. What had I said? What was she going to say? What would happen next? I thought I would die of suspense. Miss Floyd had turned back towards the window. She did not look at me again. She waved one hand towards the door. 'I shall discuss this conversation with your parents. You may go.'

I walked out, at once exhilarated and appalled at my daring. It had been so easy. I should have done it years before; then I could have avoided O-levels. Everyone should do it. That I had dared to speak to the headmistress in such a way confirmed my previously unrecognized contempt for the staff, and I ran towards the bus station smirking with satisfaction. I would do my A-levels at home. Mummy could teach me Latin, and Daddy could do English and history. It would be much more fun than going to school.

181

I walked home from Aylthorpe, where the bus dropped me, wrapped in rosy plans for my new, free life. I would be helpful to Mummy and Daddy, of course. I would get up early and drive the boys to school before settling at the kitchen table to read about the Reformation with Daddy. I would write essays in the afternoon before collecting the boys, and I would study Latin when they were doing their prep. Mummy and Daddy would see the sense of this. At the end of the drive I quickened my step, eager to reach home and tell them.

Mummy was leaning against the Aga, her hands on her hips, looking on sightlessly as the cat Angelica crouched on the floor, batting a limp dead mouse between her paws.

'You're back early,' said Mummy when she saw me. 'Are you all right?'

'Fine,' I said brightly, edging towards the kettle. As soon as I saw Mummy, my plan became absurd. She was not going to see it my way. 'Where's Daddy?' I was playing for time. Skipping around the kitchen as if on springs, I made toast and uncharacteristically offered some to Mummy.

She didn't notice anything untoward. She slumped in a chair, resting her head in her hands. 'Darling, I have some very serious news. Helen is in hospital; she's extremely ill. Daddy has gone to see her with Liza. We should hear something this evening.'

'God, how awful. Will she be all right?'

Mummy shook her head. 'I just don't know. It's to do with her liver, and Liza is terribly worried.'

I pulled a chair forward, tumbling a sleeping cat to the floor, and sat down opposite Mummy. I tried to think about Helen, but my head was too full of my own news, and nothing could rest in my brain until I had confessed.

'I've left school,' I said baldly.

'Don't be so ridiculous. You can't leave school, you aren't old enough to. What has given you this idea?'

She was angry. I wished more than anything that I could unsay the words, all the stupid arrogant words I had uttered that day. But it was too late, and I had a penitent urge to tell all and somehow be absolved.

Mummy paced round the kitchen. Her face sagged and she looked old. Lines I had never seen before were etched into the pallor around her eyes and mouth.

'I told Miss Floyd that I have no respect for the teachers and that I want to do my A-levels from home.'

'Well, that was bloody stupid.' Mummy picked up the hair-brush, glaring into the mirror as she pounded her scalp. 'Not to mention downright rude.' Her hair fanned crackling outrage. 'You will go to school and do your A-levels there and that is that. You must ring Miss Floyd and apologize at once.'

She was right, but an evil pride within me would not let me back down. 'No, I will not,' I said. 'I'm never going back there, and I'm not staying here either. You are so narrow-minded. You think that school is the best thing ever, and it's not. I hate it and I hate you.'

I stormed out and ran down the drive. Then I couldn't think of anywhere to go or anything to do. I caught sight of the telephone-box, found a coin in my pocket, and rang Merry-Curl. Trying to keep my voice level and relaxed, I asked

183

him to come and pick me up. 'I've just passed my driving test, so we've got to celebrate.'

Merry-Curl was surprised. 'It's only half-past four,' he pointed out. 'Where can we celebrate now?'

I abandoned my pretence. 'Oh please, James, come and get me and I'll explain. I've done something awful.'

Merry-Curl duly arrived, but not before I had spent five minutes skulking behind the phone-box to dodge Mummy when she passed on her way to Aylthorpe to collect the boys from the bus.

Merry-Curl listened to my explanation in shocked silence, then he laughed. 'Let's go to Cromer for fish and chips.' He sniggered as we drove. 'I'm not surprised Eleanor was angry.' His companionable use of her name jarred. 'You've got to go home and apologize. How could you ever have thought you would get away with it?' And he laughed, his eyes closing into little slits in his face.

I felt utterly, self-pityingly alone. Merry-Curl was supposed to be my friend, and even he made no effort to see my point of view. Exhausted and defeated, I agreed to apologize. 'But let's not go back yet. I'd like to learn how to play snooker,' I said untruthfully, cravenly seeking delay. Merry-Curl, still chortling to himself from time to time, beat me in three games and bored me into a stupor by explaining all the rules of snooker. I escaped to the loo, and he took on the pub champion. At ten o'clock we left.

Back at Mildney I prevaricated. 'James, you go in, I've just got to get something from my bedroom.' I pushed open the front door and ran upstairs. Merry-Curl went through into the kitchen. I opened my bedroom door and turned on the light. In the bed, head muffled beneath the pillow, a figure was curled in sleep. I couldn't see who it was, and no clue was offered among my strewn clothes on the floor. Silently I backed out of the room and turned off the light. 'How dare they, how dare they,' I hissed to myself as I ran down the stairs, fear lost in a bubbling pit of indignation.

'Where am I supposed to sleep?' I demanded angrily as I entered the kitchen. 'There's someone in my bed. Get them out now.' I slammed the door and aimed a kick at a purring cat.

'Va Va, why don't you shut up?' Brodie's quiet words poured over me like cold water. His eyes were pink-rimmed and strained.

Mummy spoke. 'Vinnie is in your bed. Her mother is dying. How dare you be so inconsiderate and selfish?'

And I remembered about Helen with a loathsome slap of remorse and sorrow. 'I didn't know she was that ill,' I whispered. 'I'm sorry, I'm sorry.' I bowed my head and stumbled to my mother, climbing on to her knee like a child, crying into the soft scented wool of her cardigan.

August 1990

D an's leg and its endless complications made it impossible for him to leave home. He was nineteen and had nothing to do. He hated it, but even though he was frequently in pain, he never complained or revealed it by so much as a wince. Poppy was reluctantly boarding at a girls' school where Mummy taught Latin three days a week, so Dan and Dad were alone together in the house. They spent their mornings dismantling cars. It was hot, Dan never wore a shirt and his shoulders turned deep brown beneath a chain of tattooed mermaids whose busts expanded when he flexed his muscles. Dad leant on his car, his head bowed low over the engine. Dan drove alongside and opened his own car's bonnet, and they traded parts.

'I'll swap my carburettor for that old gasket of yours,' said Dan. 'It's a good deal, I can find you a much better one.'

Dad was always taken in and always furious about it.

'I can't refuse Dan anything,' he complained to Mum, when his car had to be pushed back to the garage because its vital organs were all missing. 'He is the most consummate con-man and he breaks my heart. He'll have my wheels next.'

Dad was haunted by Dan's accident. He could not bear to visit him on the numerous occasions he was in hospital, patiently playing cards and waiting, endlessly waiting for an improvement.

I slept in a nylon bag on the floor in Brodie's attic that night, my head pressed against the black lumpy walls which hung their gloom over mine.

In a defeated monotone, Mummy had told me how Zoe had telephoned after Helen's operation. It had not worked, her liver could not be saved, and all they could do was wait. Helen's brother and sister, as well as Zoe and Daddy and Liza, were at the hospital. Mummy didn't say it, but I knew they would stay there until she died. Vinnie had been told how ill her mother was, but she had come to Mildney with Nat, Helen's small baby, too confused and shattered to be able to cope with the unfamiliar surroundings of the hospital room. Mildney was no safer haven. Each room glared grief and memory from dusty corners where I could picture Helen standing, laughing, or stubbing her cigarette out and then guiltily rubbing the carpet. The image of her dying in hospital in a metal bed with her family grouped around her flitted in and out of my head. I slept fitfully and uneasily.

Only Dan and Poppy went to school the next day. Brodie, Flook and I were determined to be at home with Mummy and

Vinnie. After breakfast, I shut myself in the cloakroom with the telephone and rang Miss Floyd. I hoped she couldn't hear my heart thudding in my throat as I spoke. 'Miss Floyd, this is Gabriella Lincoln. I have to apologize for what I said yesterday. I am sorry I was rude and disrespectful, and what I said was not true.' I paused, and there was a horrible, black silence; I hurried on. 'I know you wish to take the matter to my parents, but something awful has happened, and however much I deserve punishment, my parents cannot be bothered with the matter at present, so please, *please* don't bring it up with them.'

And Miss Floyd, as I knew she would but hoped against hope that she wouldn't, asked, 'And what exactly is this awful thing, Gabriella?' Her question, cold and hard, rattled towards me like a marble on glass.

'My half-sister Helen is very ill,' I said. 'My father is at the hospital now, and my mother is looking after her little boy.' My ear was hot and bruised by the phone pressed against it. Relief and blood rushed to the rest of my head when Miss Floyd said, 'Very well. I do not intend to let the matter rest, but for the moment I shall refrain from writing to your parents. It is up to you, Gabriella, to make amends.'

'Thank you, Miss Floyd.' I put the phone down, praising God in His wisdom for making her forget to ask why I was not at school.

I told Mummy I had done it, and she smiled and hugged me. 'Well done. I'm proud of you, and it takes one weight off my mind.'

The day crawled into afternoon. Vinnie prowled up and down the house like a caged animal, not speaking, not eating, endlessly checking the telephone to see if it was working. Whenever it rang, she stopped and stood at bay, her wide eyes ready to absorb shock. Mummy went to collect Poppy and Dan at tea-time. 'Look after Vinnie,' she whispered as she left.

Ten minutes later the phone jangled, clarion and demanding. It was Zoe. 'Is Eleanor there?'

'No, she's gone to Aylthorpe.'

'Mum's dead.' Zoe's voice came from a million miles away, echoing, alone. 'I've got to tell Vinnie.' I nodded and passed the phone to Vinnie.

I did not know what to do, so I went out of the room to give Vinnie privacy. A moment later a deep howl came rolling up and up until it was a scream. Vinnie couldn't stop. Until Mummy returned I stood hugging her. Brodie and Flook hovered at her side, holding her hands as great shudders passed through her and she went on howling. She was like someone in a trance, unaware of anything around her. Agony broke out of Vinnie and splintered into all of us, but Brodie, Flook and I were numb. Our sorrow was for Vinnie and we could feel nothing else.

Much later, when Vinnie had fallen asleep, exhausted, I went with Mummy to collect Daddy and Liza and Zoe. I was almost afraid to look at them as they came out to the car together. Liza and Zoe leaned on each other's arms, not speaking. Daddy walked with his shoulders set awkwardly and his steps halting, like a man on the moon, or a soul lost in limbo. No one spoke. As we drove home, I saw Daddy's face beside me. It was lit grey and stony by the street-lamps, his eyes staring at nothing, while silent tears poured down his cheeks.

*   *   *

A week later Helen was buried at a tiny church by a stream near Liza's house. The churchyard was bright with daffodils, and the wet flint walls dripped velvet grey, soft as a donkey's nose. Blossom drifted like macabre confetti on the spring breeze and mocked the herd of weeping mourners as we followed the coffin out into the churchyard. Hypnotized, I saw Helen in her neat box swing down into the grave and rest deep in black earth. Daddy and Liza huddled together supporting each other, tiny above the gaping wound in their lives. I held Mummy's hand and pushed my face into her coat, not wanting to see or touch grief, not wanting to know pain, longing to turn back time and be safe again.

The day after the funeral, I took Mummy to Norwich. Aided by prescribed opiates, she passed her driving test. It was the twenty-fourth time she had taken it.

February 1991

I came home for Dad's seventy-eighth birthday. February was flat and grey, and Mildney smouldered around its fireplaces, wells of bright warmth linked by empty passages where your breath frosted the air. Dad had been in hospital for a few days after having sudden torrential nosebleeds. In hospital he exasperated the doctors by refusing to wear a name tag. 'I know who I am,' he stated, summoning dignity to his prone position. He had more success with the nurses, and quoted Housman to them as they chivvied him like a child through the dreary daily routine. He came home weary, and slept a lot in his old armchair in front of the playroom fire. Waking, he reached down to the piles of books and boxes at his side. He collected junk like a jackdaw and arranged his spoils in old shoeboxes, sifting through them for hours on end. He made a necklace to hang over the mantelpiece by joining a silver-plated elephant to a tiny sword on a thread of copper wire and a watchstrap out of folded masking tape and bicycle chain.

When I arrived from London he greeted me with a mocking smile. 'You look tired, love. Playing too hard, I suspect. Or could you have been working?'

He loved to hear detailed explanations of our lives, and leaned forward, listening and nodding, interrupting with his own anecdotes. For his birthday, I had brought a Rolls-Royce. I had been lent it to test-drive for a television programme. Dad laughed and clapped his hands. 'Let's take it out and show it Norfolk,' he said. Leaning on his stick, he walked out to the car. 'Get the hood up,' Dad demanded, and I fumbled for the catch, praying that he wouldn't insist on sticking a twig into the carburettor or implementing any of his other practical improvements for recalcitrant cars. He stared into the gleaming silver engine. 'What a beautiful sight. A piece of perfection.' He blew his nose and got into the car. We swooped off down the drive, Dad in full flow about driving a racing car across Arizona in the forties. He insisted on taking the wheel, and I plunged back in the seat and stifled a moan of horror as he skidded on to a bank past an advancing tractor, revving the haughty, silent engine to Neanderthal squeals.

'I'll drop you in Aylthorpe and you can get me a paper. I want to take this machine down to the garage. Mr Watts will love it.' Dad's eyes sparkled. We screeched into Aylthorpe on two wheels. Dad stopped by a newsagent's shop. I began to get out. Before my feet were on the ground I was forgotten; Dad put his foot down and sped away. I bounced off the squashy seat and fell sprawling on the tarmac. Shaking, laughing hysterically, I picked myself up. I couldn't believe he had done it. He could have killed me.

Moments later he was back. 'Jump in, love, we're going home.'

He denied all knowledge of my fall from the car. 'No, darling. Really? I couldn't have done that to you.'

Birthday tea was an orgy of chocolate cake and presents. Dad opened them with childish glee. The hot-water bottle clad in a Ninja Turtle outfit was a big hit, and afterwards Dad dozed, exhausted, his cheek resting on Donatello's beaming face. Mum and Poppy, home from school to revise for her 'mocks', went to collect the boys from the station and Dan from a friend's house. I started to cook supper. Half an hour later, I went into the playroom. Dad was still asleep but his face was parchment white, and a terrible black stream of blood oozed from his nose. Panic froze me in the doorway. Dad woke with a start and, hunched in his chair, pressed the fabric of the hot-water bottle cover to his face. I brought him wads of loo paper and sat with him. He tried to speak, but blood came out of his mouth. My cat Angelica, never one to miss an opportunity, leapt up and started licking the blood-soaked chair.

'You fiend!' I hauled her out of the room. Dad coughed. He looked miserable and macabre. I rang the doctor. An ambulance arrived. Dad was still bleeding, the playroom was a battlefield; strewn toys had caught drips of blood and lay like corpses on the carpet. I kicked them out of sight, drivelling non-conversation at Dad. He couldn't answer. Waiting in the ambulance, I held his hand and my mind raced with prayers for Mum's return. She appeared at the moment the ambulance men were driving off, and leapt in. 'I'm here, Patrick, I'm here.'

I got out, shaking, and my parents drove away, blue lights flashing their path through the darkness.

In the house, Brodie, Flook and Dan sat doleful at the kitchen table, their carefully wrapped presents for Dad mocking his absence. Poppy sniffed back tears as she washed up tea plates. They looked like tiny children deprived of a treat. 'He'll be all right,' I urged. 'Mum will be a while, though. Let's go to the pub for a bit.'

'I've got Dad some champagne.' Brodie leaned his head in his hands. 'And now he's not here to drink it.' His expression had returned to infant dolour, shock denuding him of sophistication. Flook had painted a picture of Dad's Mercedes; the paint was still wet, and it glistened when it caught the light.

There was a knock at the door and Jim came in carrying a camera. 'I've brought Patrick a present,' he said. Then he saw our drawn faces. 'What's the matter?'

Poppy told him. Jim put the camera on the dresser and hugged her. 'Come on. He's as strong as an ox. He'll be back home in a day or two. Now I'm going to buy you each a drink to cheer you up and I'll stay with you till Eleanor comes back.'

Jim now seemed to feel responsible for all of us. He chivvied us like a mother hen, his eyes beady for any dawdling, as we walked down the drive to the pub. We paused on the bridge, peering through the dark of the evening into the river, searching for a silvered hint of a trout or a powder-puff duck floating past. We saw nothing save our heads silhouetted in moonlight, peering in line over the bridge in the gloom.

The pub was full. It was Saturday night, and a group of young farmers were prematurely celebrating the end of the filthy, mud-logged winter. Their round red faces moustached with creamy foam from their pints of beer were cheery and alien. We sat at a distant table, fiddling with beer-mats, lost for conversation. Jim was at the bar. The young farmers gurgled into song.

> 'Swing low, sweet chariot,
> Coming for to carry me home,
> Swing low, sweet chariot,
> Coming for to carry me home.'

They stopped, some still humming, but they didn't know the words. But Flook and Brodie, Dan, Poppy and I did, and we sang all the verses, at once wounded and healed by the song.

'It's my fault for letting him drive that car.' After two brandies, I was ready for some self-reproach.

Poppy was crisp. 'Rubbish. It's happened before. It was nothing to do with going out. He had a brilliant time, didn't he?'

She told the boys about Dad hurling me from the car. They laughed and, spirits flickering, we returned home. Behind the house, Jim caught sight of the Rolls-Royce. His smile gleamed in the dark. 'I used to steal those when I was a kid.'

'You didn't!' Poppy and I laughed.

'You'll never know, will you?' Jim stroked the long bonnet of the car and followed us into the house.

Mum wasn't in the kitchen; Flook charged through to the playroom. 'Dad, you're back!' he bellowed, and we herded behind him.

There was no sign of any blood. Mum and Dad were sitting

by the fire, the remains of supper on trays being devoured by cats at their feet.

Mum came out with the trays. 'He recovered as soon as we got to hospital. I think the shock of being back in the ward stopped the nosebleed. He's fine now.'

I started towards the door. 'I wouldn't go in there,' Mum warned. 'He's giving a nut-by-bolt account of the Rolls-Royce engine to the boys.' She snorted with sudden laughter. 'I don't think they're at all interested, but it's his birthday, so they think they have to pretend to be.'

A few minutes later, Dad, deceptively placid in the wheelchair the hospital had lent him, led a troop of unenthusiastic boys and Jim outside. They were going to photograph the Rolls-Royce with Dad's new camera.

After Helen died, Liza brought Vinnie and Nat, refugees with all their world in cardboard boxes and plastic bags, to live with us. As I stalked furiously through the house, searching for my slime-green PVC trousers, I felt Mildney had become a crazed doll's house. In the black attic, Brodie sat in front of a mirror, delicately Supergluing his ears to the sides of his head, a French textbook forgotten, lying spattered with sticky drips on the table. Dan and Poppy, bewildered by suddenly not being the youngest, stoutly got on with their games, sawing Action Man's legs off with a carving knife and flushing them down the loo, where they bobbed pinkly when anyone went for a pee.

Liza couldn't bear to return to the Glade alone. Shrunken by sorrow she scuttled through our house, silently materializing from empty rooms, head bowed to hide the coursing tears on her face. She followed Mummy, mirroring her actions because she couldn't remember how to function alone, and sat with Daddy, each one trying to rally the other's spirits with damp jokes.

I found my trousers under Flook's bed in a small suitcase. 'Why have you packed these? In fact, why have you packed at all?' Flook was watching *Return of the Living Dead* in the playroom. Vinnie, Nat dozing on her knee, was with him.

'I'm getting out of here.' Flook did not raise his eyes from the screen. 'There are too many people. I'm getting my own flat in Norwich as soon as I can.'

'What about school? You're not even sixteen yet.'

I too was becoming drawn into the grisly goings-on flickering across the screen; Flook's answer was plausible in the face of ghoulish spectres emerging from coffins. 'I haven't been there for six months, and no one has noticed. But don't tell Mummy.'

Admiring Flook's plan, I slumped next to him on the sofa, fantasizing my own escape from home. I wanted to live in London. Norwich was too bound up with school, and school was nearly over. I wanted a new life full of glamour.

In September Vinnie and Nat went to Canada with Liza for a long holiday, and Mummy took a job teaching Latin at a girls' school on the coast. Three times a week she drove off, legal at last, wearing sensible school clothes and her wellington boots. Not until her first pay cheque arrived did she splash out and buy some shoes. Flook hid at the bottom of the drive until he saw her depart each morning, and then he came home. One morning Daddy met him in the kitchen for elevenses. 'What are you doing here, Flook? You should be at school.'

'I don't go any more. They don't want me to, and I don't want to.' Flook's head was flung back, a twist of defiance curved his lip.

'I see.' Daddy narrowed his eyes. 'And no doubt you will be supporting yourself from now on. If you are not at school, you can get a job. Let me know if you find one you like.'

Daddy's tone was icy; Flook didn't care. 'I'll have a look around, and see what comes up,' he said airily.

Daddy lit a cigarette and threw the match on the floor. 'You will doubtless do as you please, but get on with it for Christ's sake, and stop bellyaching.'

Brodie and I were righteous, furious and jealous. Mummy was not told, and Flook went on pretending to go to school. I kept expecting him to leave home, but he was enjoying the charade and lingered on into the spring. If he had nothing better to do and the weather was bad, he did go to school, so he still had enough essays to keep Mummy's suspicions at bay. Brodie and I had exams; Flook pretended he did.

It was Tuesday. We were about to leave for school, very late. Our exams were not until the afternoon, and Daddy had agreed to lend me the car. Flook had apparently been dispatched on the bus earlier. He burst in through the kitchen door, twigs and leaves from his hiding-place in the hedge shivering on his coat.

'God, you're stupid,' I sneered at him, armed by the smugness of being only weeks away from finishing school legitimately. 'How can you be so selfish? Mummy will hit the roof.'

Flook frowned, his breath heaving, mouth set and angry. 'Daddy knows, so I don't see why you should interfere.' He moved menacingly towards me, his chin jutting defiance.

'Don't be so pathetic.' I turned away coldly. A strained roar issued from Flook, and I swung round to see him bearing down upon me, both arms raised, a motorbike helmet held like a trophy above his head. He tried to smash at me with the helmet. I grabbed a chair, edging away from him, squeaking, 'Calm down, don't be silly.' I stumbled backwards across the kitchen, dodging from side to side as Flook swung his bludgeon through the air. I thought it would never end, and wondered if I should allow him to hit me. I had a faint hope that contrition would calm him and I enjoyed the prospect of forgiving him.

I lowered my guard and Flook charged. He never reached me. A metal dustbin descended over his head, arresting his progress. Brodie, displaying unexpected stealth, had crept towards the rubbish while Flook and I were duelling. Tipping a suppurating heap of tea-leaves, eggshells and slithering wine bottles on the floor, he ambushed Flook with the bin. Echoing rage boiled in the bin for a few moments. Then there was silence. We cautiously eased Flook out and found him laughing.

Churches, solid Norman towers, sky-scraping spires and ancient Saxon round towers stand tall on Norfolk's damp earth, and they haunted Patrick. Walking through dark medieval woods a mile from Mildney he found the scrambled walls of a ruined chapel, its columns and figures scattered among brambles, untouched since vandals plundered it. He took the children there, and they clutched his coat and hid when they came to a hidden lake. Patrick pointed to the tips of beech trees, bursting out at knee-height. The rest of the trees had been swallowed by the lake. The pagan spell of the woods, where a gibbet displayed a gruesome tally of weasels, rabbits and the red smear of a fox, terrified and enchanted Va Va, and the sight of a stone head rolling in dead leaves by the chapel fuelled bedtime stories for weeks afterwards.

Driving along narrow, mud-brown lanes, Patrick used churches to guide him through the countryside. When he reached the coast he parked the car on the edge of the cliff and Va Va, Brodie and Flook rushed to buy ice lollies, their chemical red, blue and electric pink the only colours in a panorama of iron skies and steel-dark sea. Teeth turned the colour of the lollies as Patrick told the children sea stories: of Harold Hardrada and Sir Cloudesley Shovell; of a church bell ringing still in the deep North Sea, the ghostly peal commemorating the terrible day when the church of Dellingford and its congregation slipped off the crumbling cliff and perished beneath the waves.

Va Va loved the Jewel Church best. The round flint tower had windows like arrow slits at the top, and a tomb of marble stood alone in the empty nave. The tomb was decorated with a huge polished stone; Va Va thought it was a rare jewel, bigger than any other ever mined. Eleanor had told her a story about a Blue Prince, and she imagined him buried there, sleeping for ever, wrapped in glamorous ossified youth, a fit bridegroom for Sleeping Beauty.

Va Va was deep in a religious phase. Every Sunday she went to church, alone or with a weekend guest she had cajoled into accompanying her. She loved the orderliness and ritual of the church; the neat rows of pews with tapestry hassocks plump and square beneath them; the crimson hymn-books which never had pages missing, so that it was a joy to turn to the page announced on white cards on the wall. The vicar was boring. Each Sunday he read a different sermon in the same grey monotone. Va Va didn't understand why he read such dull texts. At home, Patrick told her stories about the saints and made her laugh with silly voices and faces. In church everyone fidgeted and some even slept.

Patrick and Eleanor were relieved when Va Va's interest in the Sunday service waned and she no longer pestered Eleanor to iron her dress, or Patrick (in the absence of someone less used to her wiles) to go with her.

August 1991

T he summer Dad was ill, we went often to Sall Church. It has the tallest tower in Norfolk and its high vaulted ceiling and delicate columns are unexpected in a rural church. Anne Boleyn's ghost haunts it and so do a thousand others. Up a steep stone stairway off the nave there is a whispering gallery. Gargoyles grin down from the ceiling like stars, orbiting the central sinister face of the Green Man.

Dad found walking a great strain, and sat in the pews contemplating the altar and the great yew tree which swirled behind it through warped green diamond panes of glass.

He and I had many outings, and they filled me with nostalgia for my childhood. Dad was very proud; he never complained about his illness, and I caught his courage and submerged my sadness and my fear. Life's circle felt smugly, horribly complete now as I, not he, drove a large car along narrow lanes, while he, not I, sat in the back and called for lemonade. But Dad made it impossible and impertinent to be sad. His verve and his pleasure in the landscape welled over into me, and we drove slowly, admiring a line of slender poplars stalking a grey skyline, or a great beechwood canopying us in underwater light. Dad existed in a state of perpetual worship of the beauty of the countryside, combined with a sense of the ridiculous.

'The Norfolk landscape sends a shiver through my soul,' he said. 'It really is exquisite, is it not, my love?' Seconds later he sighed, and in a voice buoyant with mirth said, 'I say, I really am a crashing old bore, aren't I? Shut up, Patrick, for Christ's sake.'

We reached a café at tea-time to be told that it was closed. Dad, dark glasses and fisherman's cap making him look like a spy on holiday, laughed. 'Ha, it's sublime! What can one expect from a hole like this!'

The po-faced proprietor continued to sweep the floor. Dad advanced, his faded blue eyes melting with charm as he sweetened his voice to ask, 'My dear fellow, may I have the honour of sitting outside your establishment for a moment and drinking a glass of your water?'

The proprietor gave up, put down his broom, and two minutes later Dad was sitting, wickedly delighted, behind a pot of tea and a plate of uninspired cakes.

We were in Balton, a godforsaken village framed by scattered caravans which looked as if they had been taken up by the wind and hurled, cars and deck chairs sprawling beside them, against the few stubby hedges. Balton was a pit-stop during the hunt for a Ford Cortina.

Dad's Mercedes had come back with him from an Italian trip five years earlier hot and shuddering like a racehorse. Dad had driven from Assisi without stopping and the Mercedes responded gallantly until it reached our drive. There it stopped and died. Dad fiddled with the engine to no avail and the car was heaved by all my brothers as its pallbearers to its grave in the barn. With dignity it stood there, rotting and rusting but still beautiful. No scrap men were allowed to touch Sadie Bens; Dad had plans for her. On a good day he was sure it wouldn't take much to get her on the road again; on a bad day she was earmarked as his hearse.

'I shall be buried in my Mercedes,' he said, stroking the dust from her flank and polishing her star with his red spotted handkerchief.

When Sadie Benz perished Dad had replaced her with a souped-up Ford with customized wheels. Other Fords followed annually, and now we were looking for this year's model. Dad was feeling rich and jubilant, having taken three hundred pounds out of the bank to buy a car. The money was burning a hole in his pocket and the quest thrilled him. We set off with Jim, who had moved on from dam-building and was constructing a river-view seat for Dad from the skeleton of an oak tree. Jim was our expert on engines. It was his lot to damp the fanciful urges Dad and I had for every Ford Cortina we saw parked in a drive or speeding along the road. By evening we had covered eighty miles and Jim's veil of diplomacy was wearing thin.

We arrived at a council estate and penetrated the Legoland streets to a central point which was marked by a golden car. Dad and I were adamant that we should not return home empty-handed and were sure that this Cortina was our Grail. The guardian of the golden car was a young man with no shirt; his back was tattooed with an intricate and lavish portrait of his wife Leila. As his muscles moved beneath the skin, Leila winked and smiled at Dad and me; he and I were hovering, dumb with admiration, while Jim conducted the deal.

My father drove his new Cortina home, skidding round the hairpin bends to Mildney. The car gave him freedom and became his salon. For the rest of the summer he conducted all conversations from its brown nylon seats and invited his children on perilous journeys which we dreaded but dared not spurn in case he broke down and was left stranded, alone.

M erry-Curl was living in London. He had left university and was looking for a job. I went to stay with him one weekend, and found him resplendent in a long-corridored flat above the King's Road. The drawing-room swaggered beneath mighty red silk curtains and every surface was scattered with cigarette ash. Dazzled, I fell in love with him. Merry-Curl was taken aback. After an hour or two of red-faced fumbling, we went out and walked in the rain across Hyde Park and he held my hand.

In the evening, we climbed into a taxi and ticked across London to Soho for a party. Sandwiched between two strip-joints was a huge green metal door. We went in, and up and up. On the roof, spotlights draped in yellow and pink gauze cast hazy beams towards the night sky. The party was being given by one of Merry-Curl's friends from Oxford, and everyone there knew him and wanted to know who I was. Intoxicated by pink champagne and attention, I danced on the slate rooftop and promised myself that as soon as my last exam was done I would move to London.

A tall girl, with a slender cylinder body and a silver mini-dress, asked where I lived. 'Norfolk,' I replied, wishing I could have said 'Chelsea' or 'Bohemia' or anywhere exotic. 'Mansions or Square?' Her fishbowl eyes swivelled frantically and focused on me again. 'County, actually,' I admitted regretfully. She shrieked, arching her back, rippling laughter down her long white throat.

'Why don't you come and live with me? Norfolk's so far away. I've got a spare room in my flat.'

Nodding, beaming, I agreed. Merry-Curl came over and led me away. In the taxi on the way back to his flat, I realized I hadn't asked the girl her name.

Returning to Norfolk on the coach did not match my new vision of myself and my life. I reached Mildney hot and nauseated by petrol fumes. I felt frustrated, frumpy, hung-over and fed up. Daddy observed my glazed, tired eyes and my scowl. 'Burning the candle at all four corners,' he mocked, raising his eyebrows at Brodie when I flounced out of the room.

Home. Place of revision. Crowded ants' nest infested with the lowest form of life. Squalid and not at all aesthetic. I lay in my bed and thought dark thoughts until I fell asleep.

A month later, my exams were over. I didn't care whether or not I had passed them because a friend of Merry-Curl's had offered me a job running errands for a film crew working on a documentary. I was moving to London. Merry-Curl had identified the blonde cylinder girl as Palladia MacAdam, a name of unqualified sophistication in my eyes, and of gross pretension in the view of my family. Even Dan managed a Latin pun: *Et in Palladia ego*, he proffered during the 'humiliate Va Va' session the boys had the morning before I left. Daddy answered her telephone call when she rang up to confirm her offer of a room. 'Your father is divine,' she warbled, enraging me. 'And his poetry . . . heaven, absolute heaven. We shall read it together over breakfast.'

'Mmm . . .' I was unenthusiastic, but perked up when Palladia told me I would have a telephone next to my bed.

Mummy became sentimental and kept following me around the house as I packed, offering broken china animals. 'This was yours when you were five; I think you should take it with you.' When I rejected the limbless pony, she folded her hands and started to recall the labour pains she suffered to bring me into the world all those eighteen years ago.

Snapping and snarling at everyone, I heaped the brown Ford Cortina with all my belongings. Daddy had given me this car as a leaving-home present. I wished it was a sports car and hardly managed to say thank you. Poppy stumbled out of the house wearing a pair of gold-painted stilettos I had thrown at her while clearing my bedroom. 'You said I could have them, I know you did,' she pleaded, rocking forward as she struggled to keep them on her feet. I couldn't be bothered to argue. Looking at her, I suddenly wanted to change my mind; to unpack the car again and stay at home. I sat down on the grass, pulling Poppy down next to me, and hugged her awkwardly. She was ten, too big to cuddle on my knee, but I remembered her baby embraces, and I wanted them again now.

Brodie and Flook came out, each carrying a slumped cat. 'We've given them their sleeping-pills. The vet says they'll work for four hours, so you should get there.' Brodie passed me the soft heap of Angelica, my ginger cat. Flook lifted Witton, the stripy one, into the car, placing him carefully inside a hat where he fitted like coiled rope.

It was time to go. I hugged everyone in turn and, shaking, crawled into the tiny space left by my luggage. Mummy and Daddy, Brodie, Flook, Dan and Poppy stood by the porch waving as I grated the gears and drove away down the drive. I cried all the way to Norwich, but when I jerked into the slow lane of the London road, I became a new person. Super-efficient and grandly independent, I chugged to London, my top speed downhill a stately forty. The cats woke up at Hyde Park Corner and were very alarmed. Climbing on to my shoulders and scrambling along the dashboard, they looked out at the whirling, grinding traffic and miaowed pitifully. I felt ashamed for having brought them.

October 1991

The longer I lived away from Mildney, the more often I returned. Each time I came home, I was reassured by Dad's enthusiastic discussions of fourteenth-century Chinese physics, and his determined battle against Mum's use of the categorical imperative. 'You are your mother's daughter,' he told me over and over again as I marshalled him on excursions, bossily insisting on his wearing a hat. He complained, astonished, when I refused to let him drive for thirty miles when he was recuperating from pneumonia.

In London during the week, I developed a paranoid dread of the telephone. If it rang very early or very late, I raced to answer it, rehearsing my reaction when I was told Dad had died. I knew my lines inside out. I knew how I would watch over my brothers and my sister and help them. I knew how I would speak to my mother. I knew I could cope. In London, with none of my family about me, I was ready for Dad to die.

In Norfolk, I was guilty and appalled, shocked that I could overreact so when away. There was Dad, joking and teasing, waking Mum up at dawn for a verbal sword fight over Kipling's syntax or whether Hitler invented the VW Beetle.

One weekend he was in hospital. I went to visit him with Mum. I was tired out and feeling ugly. I had impetigo. 'Impetigo is the twentieth-century descendant of the plague,' Dad announced when I arrived. 'I have asked Nurse Amalasontha, and she tells me this is so.' I glared at him and whispered to Mum, 'Is the nurse really called Amalasontha?'

'Of course not, she's called Joan, but your father is trying to change all their names here. He's persuaded the doctor to call her Amalasontha.'

Nurse Amalasontha bustled in with a cup of tea in her chubby hands. She frisked and flirted with Dad. Her gait changed from the stately glide of a ministering angel and she skittered about like an awkward heifer.

'They'll let me out of here tomorrow,' whispered Dad when Amalasontha had swerved out again. 'If they don't, I'll hitch-hike.'

At Mildney, Dan shivered in the playroom. It wasn't cold and he was wearing a jersey. He whispered to me to follow him and he limped into the hall. 'Jim's in trouble,' he said. 'The police are after him.'

'Why? What's he done?' I whispered back. 'Is it serious?'

'Very. I can't tell you why, but you should say goodbye to him. He's going to vanish any day now, before they find him, and he won't say where.'

I begged and cajoled, bullied and wheedled, but Dan wouldn't tell me what Jim had done. I tried for clues: 'Does Dad know what it is?'

'Yes, but he won't tell you. Honestly, Va Va, it's no joke. It's life and death.'

'Well, it can't be that bad, or Dad wouldn't be friends with him.'

'Depends what you think is bad,' said Dan provokingly. I wondered if I should pull his hair and torture it out of him, but he was too big now.

Suddenly, he capitulated. Dan had never been good at hiding things; he always confessed when he broke a window with a cricket ball, or pinched half of Dad's engine for his car.

'Have you never guessed or wondered where Jim's money comes from?' Excitement broke over his face. I held my breath. Dan pulled me nearer and whispered in my ear, 'He's a bank robber.'

Danger, danger, glamorous, wonderful, shocking danger bolted through me. 'He didn't hurt anyone, did he?' I was anxious that the image should be untarnished. Jim, dispenser of good to the poor and needy, must have no blots on his copybook.

'No. But he did have guns,' said Dan, 'and he says the police are on to him.'

I was smiling to myself, beguiled by the notion, absurdly ignorant of any reality. 'Maybe he'll escape.' Unintentionally I began to hum, 'My daddy was a bank robber. He never hurt nobody', a song by The Clash which Brodie and I had played as teenagers.

'I don't think so.' Dan was serious. 'He will if he can disappear soon. But he thinks they are following him now.'

I flew to Italy the next morning to research a documentary about a woman who had once been married to a bank robber.

Serena Montepulchro lived among pink marble columns and white peacocks in a remote Sicilian palazzo where the top-floor rooms lay naked beneath the sky. She talked reluctantly, hiding her few words behind a thick and undoubtedly phoney Italian accent, as I followed with my tape recorder through vines and lilies. I returned to London elated. On my last night at the palazzo, Serena had imbibed half a bottle of Cente Herbe, a poison-green liqueur, and had rolled across her dining-room floor, a crazed dervish in cream lace, lobbing lumps of bread at her guests and singing along to Roy Orbison's 'Pretty Woman'. The image was unforgettable, and for once I felt like a real professional, with something to say.

There was nobody at my flat when I returned from Italy, and I had no keys. Stripping off the beautiful white cashmere shorts I had bought in Florence to celebrate my successful interview, I climbed over the porch, a kinky cat-burglar in black tights and leotard. The telephone was ringing, and with each peal I scrambled more frantically. Finally I was in, through the bathroom window; I fell inelegantly, my head just missing the lavatory bowl. The phone was still ringing. Out of breath and giggly, I picked it up. It was Flook.

'Va Va. You're back. Is anyone there?'

'Nope. Just me and the loo. I got stuck and—'

'Va Va. I've got some bad news.'

Flook's voice was rigid and tight, so heavy it seemed to fall down the line, shattering my mind. I knew.

'Dad's dead, isn't he?'

'Yes, I'm sorry I had to be the one to tell you.' Flook talked on, giving details which swam round and round, lashing my heart. 'It was last night at about seven o'clock. He wasn't in pain. He was at home.'

Suddenly cold, my teeth chattered against the phone. I listened. So many times, in so many ways, I had anticipated this. Now all the careful preparation was useless.

It's happened. He's gone now. It's happened. My brain thudded, over and over again. Flook told me to get a taxi to the station. 'We'll all go home together,' he said.

Like a sleep-walker, I obeyed his patient, simple instructions, collecting sheaves of black clothes, heaping them into a dustbin bag because my case was full from Italy. I called a cab. I was still wearing only tights and a leotard; Flook had not known this, so had neglected to tell me to get dressed. I did not think of it myself.

There followed the slowest days of my life. Minutes spiralled, never turning into hours as we went through the curious, secret rituals which death brings. Dad died on the day the clocks went back, a day he had always hated for its dismal acceptance of winter. And winter arrived, bringing sharp bright days which faded early, the sky red behind shivering black trees denuded by flint-sharp wind.

Pucker's, the undertakers, bustled into action. They laid Dad out in their breeze-block Chapel of Rest; when empty of death it doubled up as an electrician's workshop. Fearful, but unable to stay away, Poppy, Brodie and I went with Mum to see Dad there. Trussed in white satin frills like a babe prepared for christening, he lay in a silk-lined coffin. I kissed his forehead. He was colder

215

than stone. Brodie cried. Poppy, Mum and I stood dry-eyed, absorbing every detail. I didn't feel he was there. Dad would never wear white frills. He had to be somewhere else, in his fisherman's cap and old suede jacket, laughing at his corpse.

Pucker's telephoned the next morning. They had decided I was in charge, and having asked my name, clung to it.

'Hello, is that Mrs Gabrielly? Pucker's here. We just wondered if you would like the grave dug double deep?'

'What for? I don't know anything about graves.'

'Well, in case you want to pop your Mum in later.' Mrs Pucker's voice was a mixture of brisk practicality and motherly sympathy.

My knees buckled, and I agreed. 'Oh yes. Whatever you think is best. I don't think I'll ask her now though.' I told Mum later, and she doubled up with laughter.

We, her children, hovered around her, trying anything, everything, to protect her from loss, and knowing we could do nothing.

A friend brought six little brown bottles of Rescue Remedy; they were labelled for each of us. 'What's the difference between them?' Dan wondered. He took a drop from each. 'Mum's is neat brandy, Va Va's is water, and mine tastes like Coca-Cola. Who wants to swap?' He was sent outside to gather wood.

Preparing for a funeral is like making party arrangements with a knife in your spine. This, with obituaries and letters from long-ago friends, was like one of Dad's book launches. A hundred times I opened my mouth to say, 'I must show this to Dad,' only to close it foolishly.

The day before the funeral Jim arrived. Mum had chosen him to be one of the pallbearers, along with the boys and Dominic, who had arrived with Liza. 'Dan, will you ring him and ask him for me?' she said. 'Patrick loved him so much, I think he is the right person, don't you?'

'He may have gone away,' said Dan, but when he phoned, Jim was there. 'I couldn't go when I heard about Patrick. I wanted to see you lot were all right and to come to his funeral. I am deeply honoured. Tell Eleanor that of course I will be a pallbearer, no matter what.'

Dan relayed the news to Mum, and the rest of us sneaked into the Drinking Room.

'Mum doesn't know, does she?' Brodie stroked the Chinese dog on the mantelpiece.

Flook shook his head. 'We'd better not tell her till afterwards, she'll only worry.'

'Will she be angry?' asked Poppy. 'It would be awful if she wished she hadn't chosen him.'

'No. She'll like it. Dad would love it anyway, and he knew,' I said.

Dad's funeral was held on All Souls' Day. A Saturday. The day of the Rugby International Final between England and Australia. Kick-off was at three o'clock. We walked up to the church behind the hearse. Our dog T-Shirt came with us, a purple scarf tied round his hairy throat. The boys and Jim, sombre in long black coats, their eyes downcast in faces where sorrow was carved as deep as Jim's scar, lifted the coffin out of the hearse. The graveyard was full of people.

No one moved or spoke as the boys carried their father to the church.

The service began. When Nile, the dreadlocked Ghanaian singer in Brodie's band, sang 'Swing Low, Sweet Chariot' in our village church, televisions in pubs and sitting-rooms all over England roared the same words from the lips of a thousand thousand rugger fans.

> 'If you get there before I do
> Coming for to carry me home
> Tell all my friends that I'll be coming soon
> Coming for to carry me home.

> 'Swing Low, sweet chariot
> Coming for to carry me home . . .'

Twelve squad cars, six motorbikes, three vans and a helicopter were used in the raid on Jim's house. An army of men in bulletproof boiler-suits and black helmets burst in through doors and windows as Jim slept. Outside, a frogman bobbed in the duckpond, slime dripping from his rubber suit. Jim was taken away in handcuffs. The police emptied drawers, slit mattresses and pulled up floorboards. They dug up the lawn and had to re-lay it when Jim's landlord turned up to mend a barn. They rootled through three tons of hay and grain, they dismantled the car and the fridge and the cooker. They did not find what they were looking for. My father would have laughed if he had known.